*Finding peace where
she didn't think to look...*

ANNE MARIE BENNETT

Published by KaleidoSoul Media
PO Box 745, Beverly MA 01915

Book design & illustration by Carol Coogan.
www.carolcoogandesign.com

Dedication

For Jordan, Jason, Aubree,
Tori, Lissy, Shane,
Camden, Wesley, and Elle.

*May you always seek out places
where you are welcomed just as you are.*

Contents

CHAPTER 1` 1

CHAPTER 2 12

CHAPTER 3 22

CHAPTER 4 31

CHAPTER 5 39

CHAPTER 6 54

CHAPTER 7 60

CHAPTER 8 68

CHAPTER 9 82

CHAPTER 10 88

CHAPTER 11 103

CHAPTER 12 109

CHAPTER 13 116

CHAPTER 14 132

CHAPTER 15 143

CHAPTER 16 149

Journaling & Discussion Questions 152

Acknowledgements 154

About the Author 159

CHAPTER 1

Casey Donovan slouched on a bare metal folding chair in a corner of the Woodfield, Connecticut Police Station. Long, freckled arms folded themselves defiantly across her chest, and hair the color of antique pennies fell to her shoulders in a tangled web.

The station hummed with steady activity even though it was past midnight. People moved, coughed, laughed. Papers rustled. A siren blasted suddenly in the background. Two phones jangled at once, yet Casey felt disconnected from the activity, like an island immersed in fog. She rubbed her palms on her white shorts and glanced nervously at the front door. Her mother would be there any minute, and she would have to explain. Casey sighed and brushed the coppery bangs out of her eyes.

The others had left a few minutes ago. Eric hadn't even kissed her goodbye. Eric. She kicked the leg of the chair. If only he hadn't taken a swing at that other guy. If only he'd gone outside with her to watch the fireworks like she'd wanted, then they'd still be at the 4th-of-July party

1

at Jimmy Patterson's house on the river.

And then one swing hadn't been enough for him. By the time Casey and the others had rushed inside, Eric had the other boy pinned down on the floor and was smashing his fists into him. When the police finally arrived, Eric had calmed down and was trying to help the boy stand up.

Casey shivered in spite of the heat. It had all seemed so familiar.

The police hadn't paid much attention to Eric because the other boy was groaning and clutching his head. Casey nearly gagged, remembering the gleaming puddles of blood that were spattered all over the Patterson's thick beige carpet and blue plaid sofa.

Then the police had found the beer and drugs in the kitchen, and the party was over.

She had tried to ask Eric why he'd been fighting with the other guy, or if he had even known him before the party. But Eric had stared at her with eyes as blank as an endless tunnel. He had shut her out. Again.

"Cut the noise, will ya?" A policeman's raspy voice yanked Casey's thoughts back to the police station. She blinked, then realized she must have kicked the folding chair again.

"Sorry," she mumbled and slumped back onto the unyielding chair, hands shoved in her pockets. She didn't bother looking up.

"Is someone coming to pick you up?" the officer asked, rummaging through the papers on his desk.

"My mom will be here soon." Casey suddenly felt sick to her stomach.

He looked up at her. "You look pale, kid," he said kindly. "Are you all right?"

"I guess so." Casey stared at the floor.

"Look, nothing much is going to happen to you," he said. "You'll come in next week. You'll talk to the judge. He'll give you a little lecture . . ." Casey looked up and grimaced at his stern, authoritative expression. "Then he'll let you go with a warning. Your boyfriend, now, he's the one in trouble. Might have to do a delinquency term this time. This isn't his first offense." He went back to his paperwork.

Casey chewed a ragged hangnail on her thumb. She couldn't bear to think of Eric, her exciting, dark-haired Eric, in prison. Then she thought of something else and her stomach lurched again. She sat on her hands and wet her lips nervously. "It's not my first offense either."

"What?"

Casey leaned forward. "I've heard that lecture from the judge once already. Does that make a difference in what's going to happen to me?" Her voice wavered, and she swallowed hard.

"It might," he replied, coming over and leaning against the counter in front of her. He was a large, burly man with a fringe of fine blond hair, and his eyes were as wide and kind as a bulldog's. "What happened last time?"

"Same thing, except there wasn't a fight. Just a lot of loud noise and . . ."

"And some drugs and booze, right?"

She nodded unhappily and began to chew on the hangnail again.

He hesitated. "My boss makes all those decisions," he said, nodding in the direction of a small white-haired man in an adjoining glassed-in office. "He might let you go with a warning again, but I doubt it."

"I won't . . .have to go to jail, will I?"

He chuckled deep in his throat. "Nah, don't worry about that. But it'll probably go on your record this time."

Casey slumped back in the seat and tapped her flip-flopped foot impatiently on the floor. Mom would be furious. She hadn't had enough pain and grief this past year. Now Casey was going to add to it.

But she loved Eric. How could she not be with him, go places with him? Especially when being with him was the only thing that made her own frightening memories fade into the background?

Just then the main door to the police station opened. "I think your parents are here," the officer said as an auburn-haired woman and a tall man with sandy hair made their way down the corridor.

Casey's eyes opened wide. Parents? Had her Dad really come with her mother? She jumped up to get a closer look at the couple who by now were standing at the information desk in the main hall, their backs to her. They were talking to the officer on duty.

That's what must have taken her so long. She'd called

4

Casey's dad. Casey suddenly felt hopeful. Maybe they could just go home together afterwards and work things out.

But as soon as the couple turned and walked down the hallway toward them, Casey's hope was shattered like a bullet speeding through a funhouse mirror.

"That is not my father," Casey said to the policeman, her hands clenched at her sides.

With an amused smile, he pointed to the man's patched jeans and bright red Mickey Mouse T-shirt. "Your mom must go for the boyish type."

"He's not her boyfriend, either," Casey responded sharply. "I've never seen him before in my life."

"Okay, okay, I was only kidding," he said, moving toward the couple and greeting them. "Hi folks." He extended a large hand toward the woman. "I'm Officer Cunningham. This your girl?"

She shook his hand quickly and said, "Yes, I'm Sunny Donovan," but her eyes were on Casey. "I can't believe you did this to me again." Her voice was low and shiny-hard with anger.

"Look, I'm sorry, mom . . ." Casey began, then shook her head. Tears stung her eyelids and she longed to cry, to be held on her mother's lap, like long ago when she had accidentally slammed her fingers in the car door. But things were different now. She took a deep breath against her mother's anger. "I needed to be with Eric. You just don't understand."

Casey stared defiantly into her mother's deep brown

eyes for a moment, then looked away. She couldn't bear the disappointment that she saw there. Instead, she focused on the man in the T-shirt.

"And who the hell are you?" She steeled her tears with sarcasm.

Sunny cleared her throat. "Watch your mouth, Casey, and show some respect. This is Peter Wright, the rector at Grace Episcopal Church. Grandma Rachel and I took you there on Easter, remember?"

"Dragged me there is more like it," Casey mumbled to herself as Peter shook her hand. She vaguely remembered this man now, robed in white and gold, up front at the altar of her grandmother's church. Her mom had introduced her to him after the service and he'd seemed happy to meet her, although she couldn't figure out why. He even seemed glad to see her now, in spite of the fact that they were in a police station in the middle of the night.

"Hi Casey," Peter was saying. "It's good to see you again."

"Right." A lingering twinge of sarcasm colored her voice.

"Of course, I'd much rather see you in one of our church pews than in a police station." He grinned, trying to lighten the difficult situation.

She knew he intended to be funny, but she shrugged and looked away. This wasn't a Sunday Social, after all.

Peter hesitated. "I hope you don't mind that your mother asked me to come along. She thought maybe I could help."

"Help?" Casey folded her arms across her tight red and blue striped shirt.

"She wasn't sure what would happen since this is your second offense and all." He looked at Officer Cunningham for assistance.

The big man gestured toward the other side of the glass double doors. "Talk to Sergeant Janowicz. He makes all the big decisions around here."

Peter looked around. He saw a few officers chatting and doing paperwork. Empty cardboard coffee cups and overflowing ashtrays littered the counters and desktops. There were two men being handcuffed, then led down the corridor. "Where are the other kids?" he asked.

"They left a little while ago, but they're scheduled to appear in court a week from Monday."

Sunny tucked some loose strands of her wavy auburn hair behind her left ear. She wore denim capris and a sleeveless white shirt. A shiny, thick pink scar ran all the way from her wrist to her elbow, marring her slender arm. "Casey too?" she asked nervously, biting her bottom lip.

"Can't say for sure," Cunningham replied. He stared at the ugly scar on Sunny's arm for a few seconds, then cleared his throat. "That's up to my boss. Casey was with the others, and they found illegal drugs at the party site."

The four of them stood still for a moment, a tight tableau of tension.

Peter took charge, breaking the silence. He attempted a smile, then rubbed his hands together briskly. "Okay, ladies, let's go see Sergeant Janowicz. Nice meeting you, Officer." He shook Cunningham's hand, then steered Casey and Sunny through the glass doors and up to the Sergeant's desk.

Janowicz glanced through Casey's file and adjusted the silver-rimmed glasses on his shiny nose. "Court date, Monday the 13th. 10 a.m. sharp. Charged with causing a disturbance and illegal possession of marijuana, cocaine, and alcohol."

Sunny gasped and looked at Casey. "You didn't tell me you had—" Her voice was rising into hysteria.

Peter put his hand on Sunny's arm and spoke with a calmness that startled even Casey. "Were the drugs and alcohol actually in Casey's possession?"

Janowicz flipped through the papers again. "It doesn't say that here."

"Then the charge isn't accurate. I have a suggestion, though. Instead of wasting the court's time, how about letting Casey work with me this summer in my church?"

The Sergeant leaned his wiry body back in the big brown chair and stared doubtfully at Peter's Mickey Mouse T-shirt. "And what church would that be, exactly?"

"Grace Episcopal," Peter said. He noticed that his attire was under close scrutiny, and grinned. "Don't worry, I don't wear Mickey Mouse when I'm preaching."

The Sergeant took off his glasses and set them on the desk. "Oh, sure, my sister goes there. She speaks highly of you. Exactly what kind of church work did you have in mind for Miss Donovan?"

Peter glanced at Casey who still stood with her arms defiantly crossed over her chest. "Our Youth Group is starting work on a production of the musical *Godspell* this week. We'll be rehearsing two or three nights each week all summer plus Saturday afternoons. We could use another cast member."

"That's a wonderful idea, Peter!" Sunny said, clapping her hands once and turning to Casey. "Casey has always loved to sing, and we used to take her to musicals all the time when we were . . . when she was little. She even plays the guitar."

Janowicz nodded thoughtfully. "It does sound like a good idea—"

"Do I have a say in any of this?" Casey demanded, glaring alternately at Peter and her mother.

"Yes, you do," Janowicz said sternly. "You have a say. Here's your choice. You can go to court next Monday and take the chance that this incident will go on your record, not to mention any other sentence the judge will impose on you and your friends. Or you can thank Reverend Wright for offering you a chance to do something with your summer that's worthwhile and good for the community."

Casey was silent. She had been backed into a corner and she knew it. But the Youth Group at Grace Episcopal Church? That didn't sound like fun. She didn't know those kids at all. She would have to be an outsider. Again.

Sunny put her arm around Casey but was immediately shrugged off. "Please, Casey," she pleaded. "I don't want this to go on your record."

"But, Mom! My summer!" Fury forced out her words. "I'll be sixteen next month and you promised I could get a job." She kicked the side of the desk.

"And you promised you weren't going to see Eric anymore, remember?"

Casey backed a few steps away from the adults, loneliness burning a river of emptiness in her stomach. She was clearly defeated. "All right, all right. I'll do *Godspell* with the Youth Group this summer." She shook her head in disgust.

Her mother let out a long sigh and smiled gratefully at Peter.

Casey didn't mean to cause so many problems, but she had no idea how she was going to stand a whole summer with those church kids.

"That's settled then," the Sergeant said, quickly handing some papers across the desk to Sunny. "Sign these and you can go."

Sunny signed the papers, then reached over to shake his hand.

"Thank you, Sergeant. We appreciate this."

"No problem," Janowicz replied, sliding the papers neatly back into the folder. "Nice to see parents taking an interest. Most couldn't care less these days."

Sunny hesitated, then put her arm around Casey's bare shoulders. "Well, I care," she said softly, adamantly. Casey stood still. She longed to lean into her mother's touch but didn't dare let go of her anger.

"Nice meeting you, Sergeant," Peter said as he turned to go. "Happy Independence Day!"

Casey frowned as they left. Independence indeed. It felt more like she had been sentenced to the worst summer of her life.

CHAPTER 2

The steady drone of the air conditioner greeted Casey the next morning as she slowly awoke from a restless sleep. She lifted herself onto her left elbow and yawned, surveying the heap of clothes on the floor. Then her eyes landed on the photograph of her with her father. The picture had been taken when she was six, before their family had started coming apart.

The dream. She'd had the dream again. As it flooded her mind, she bolted from the bed and ran to the shower, grabbing a towel from the hall closet on the way. Yet even the invigorating spray of cool water could not remove the dream's power to shake her senses.

Casey angrily rubbed her wet hair with the towel, then pulled on a pair of jogging shorts and a bright yellow T-shirt. Standing at the bureau, she quickly combed her bangs, then pushed the rest of her wet, coppery hair back with a thick yellow headband. She ran her fingers swiftly over the five music boxes that sat on the bureau amidst ribbons, jewelry, bobby pins, and assorted bottles of make-up, perfume, and nail polish. Quickly, she wound each music box as far as she could twist the little silver knobs. Then she stepped back and listened to the jumbled notes careening wildly on top of one another, crashing chaotically into her senses with a violent discord that obliterated all rational thought.

Still, the dream would not go away.

She and Mom are on one side of a steep riverbank. Dad is on the other side, screaming at them to come back. He hurtles rocks and tree branches at them in angry desperation. Her mother stands still and steady, her arms flung wide, an open invitation to be wounded. Casey trembles as she crouches behind a nearby tree, looking from one parent to the other, trying to decide which one to save first.

Finally, she begins to wade through the river toward her father. The icy water numbs her with its churlish, heavy waves as she struggles to keep her head above the water. She screams to her father that she wants to help him, but the words are lost in the frenzied rush of the now raging river. He disappears in the swirling haze of fog and mist and churning water. She realizes he is no longer there. She is alone. Alone in the middle of the turbulent river. Drowning.

The dream always ended that way. Casey, alone and drowning.

The shrill of the house phone startled her back to reality. She ran to the top of the stairs and leaned against the railing as she answered it, noticing with a brief sadness that the music boxes had slowed down, calling out their final, lingering notes.

"It's Eric," said the familiar voice.

"Hi!" Casey smiled and breathed a deep sigh of relief. The dream would fade away now. It always did when she talked to Eric. She sat on the top stair. "How are you?" she asked eagerly. "Is your mom real upset or anything?"

"She just said the usual stuff."

"That's good. What about the boy you . . .? I mean, the boy who got hurt? Have you heard if he's okay?"

"What do you want me to do? Call the hospital?" he asked sarcastically.

"Well, no. I just thought you—"

"Look, I just called to say hi. Are we still on for tomorrow afternoon?"

Casey studied her ragged fingernails. "Eric, I don't think that would be a good idea right now. I mean, I want to see you and everything, but give my mom a chance to cool down, okay?"

"Yeah, sure," he replied drily. "Then I guess I'll see you in court next Monday."

She hesitated. "I . . .I won't be there."

"Why not?"

"See, my mom brought her minister with her to the police station and he . . . talked the sergeant into letting me go." Casey was feeling more uncomfortable every second. She chewed a hangnail on her ring finger, watching a drop of blood rise to the surface.

"How the hell did he do that?" Eric asked, his voice

soaked with anger.

Casey gripped the receiver tightly. "His youth group is doing a musical this summer and they said if I'd be part of it then I wouldn't have to go before the judge, so the arrest won't be put on my record."

Eric was silent. Casey leaned forward, hugging herself tensely, as though preparing for an attack. "Eric?" she whispered into the phone.

"You'd rather spend your summer with a bunch of straight-laced church kids than with me, is that it?"

She knew that tone of voice, not only from several months with Eric, but from many years of living with her father. "No! That's not true!" she cried. "You don't understand. I don't want what happened last night on my record. My mother—"

"Your mother!" Eric's words spit through the receiver like white-hot volcanic ash. "I'm sick and tired of hearing about *your mother*. So she had a husband who abused her and now she's going through a bad divorce. So what? Everyone's got problems, Casey. You think you're the only one with problems?"

She forced her trembling voice to sound cool against the heat of his anger. "No, Eric, I don't think that. I thought you understood what—"

"Oh, I understand all right. You think you're better than the rest of us, getting excused from something that *we're* going to take the rap for."

"But I didn't have a choice," Casey pleaded. She stood

up. A mirror of tears formed in her dark, gold-flecked eyes.

"Give me a break. We all have choices. You just made one."

"What do you mean?"

"I mean it's over. I'm not into relationships with girls who can't face the music."

"But I love you, Eric." Casey faced the wall, leaning against it heavily as though to absorb the strength of its hundred years of solid standing.

Eric laughed. "Sure, you love me. If you loved me, you'd help bail me out of this one, too."

"You could do the musical with me . . ."

"No way, Casey. Ain't no way on earth I'm spending *my* summer with a bunch of clean-nosed church dweebs. You can if you want to. But don't come crying to me when you get bored and lonely. I'll be gone, babe, long gone."

Suddenly there was silence, then the loud buzz of the dial tone.

Casey slowly laid the receiver back in its cradle and absent-mindedly stroked the long, knotted limb of smooth gray driftwood beside the phone on the old maple table. Grandma Rachel had little bits of driftwood all over her house. Listlessly, Casey walked downstairs. Her stomach rumbled as she entered the kitchen where bright summer sunlight streamed through the white curtained windows. She busied herself pouring cereal and mixing a new pitcher of orange juice.

But when she sat down, the reality of Eric's phone call

began to sink in. Right to the pit of her stomach. How could it be over, she wondered, pushing the golden flakes of cereal around in the milk. How could it be possible that she would never ride on Eric's motorcycle again, never feel her arms encircling his tight body, her cheek resting against his strong back, her hair whipping around their faces in the wind? How could it be possible that she would never kiss him again, or feel his rough, sure hands tracing a pattern of welcome desire on her skin?

She let the spoon drop into the bowl with a lazy splash and stared blankly at the small basket of seashells and weathered stones in the center of the table. She felt like crying but could find no tears. Only the sick feeling in her stomach that threatened to overwhelm her with its insistent, persistent churning.

She sat that way until her mother came in the back door, followed by Grandma Rachel. Casey looked up and forced a smile. "Hi, Mom," she said. "Hi, Gram." Sunny glanced at her daughter, then bit her bottom lip and immediately busied herself emptying the dishwasher. Casey thought she noticed dark shadows under her mother's eyes.

Rachel put an arm around Casey's shoulders and gently kissed her cheek. Grandma Rachel smelled of lemons and baby powder. "Mornin', Hon. How're you feeling today?"

"Okay, I guess. How was church?"

"Oh, the usual." Rachel sat down at the table. "Sunny, don't bother with those dishes now. It's too hot."

"I don't mind, Mom," Sunny said with a deliberate

17

tightness to her voice. "It's the least I can do to help out around here." She looked pointedly at Casey, then continued to pull the dishes out and put them away, with no small amount of noise.

Rachel patted Casey's hand and winked at her. "Don't worry, Hon. We'll find another chore for you to do later."

"I'm sure you will," Casey replied with a grin she didn't feel.

"Anyway, Peter was up to his usual antics today. During the sermon he used an archery target and a real bow and arrow."

"What for?" Casey picked up her spoon and began to play with the soggy cereal.

"Something about trying to be perfect all the time and how we usually fall short of our aim," Sunny replied with hardness in her voice, looking pointedly at Casey again. Sunny slammed the dishwasher door shut and set the last glass down so hard on the counter that it smashed into thousands of tiny glittering pieces. She froze for a second, looking at the broken glass. Then, covering her face, she walked quickly out of the room.

Rachel got the broom out of the closet and began sweeping up the glass. Casey moved to help her but was waved back to her seat. "Are you really okay?" Rachel asked her.

"Sure." Casey watched her grandmother carry the dustpan of broken glass to the trash can.

"You gave us all quite a scare last night, you know."

Rachel put the broom back in the closet.

"I know, Gram. I'm sorry."

"Your mom is really worried about you."

Casey slouched even further down in the handsome oak chair. She looked at her grandmother for a moment. She had white, straight, short hair, not curled or permed like so many women her age. Her eyes were a clear and vivid blue, and her skin was soft and velvety, like ripe, wrinkled peaches.

Casey hadn't really known her until they had moved in with her in October. Her father had always wanted Sunny's mother at a distance. He had wanted everyone at a distance. Yet in the last nine months, Casey and Rachel had formed a loving bond. They were each other's "onlies." Rachel's only granddaughter. Casey's only grandmother. They would remind each other of this often and share in the specialness of it.

Casey looked away from her grandmother's earnest blue eyes now. "I know she's upset with me," she said carefully. "And I said I'm sorry. Besides, I won't be seeing Eric anymore, so it won't happen again." She ran her fingers through her damp hair.

"What happened?"

Casey shrugged as if she didn't care, but her eyes betrayed her. "He called this morning. He was mad because your minister got me off the hook."

Rachel leaned over and laid her hand on Casey's pale, freckled wrist. "I'm sorry. I know you're going to miss him."

Amazement lit Casey's dark eyes. "I thought you didn't like Eric."

"It's not about liking him, Casey. It's that we don't think he's good for you."

Casey's eyes filled with tears and she brushed them haphazardly away. "But I love him, Gram. When I was with him, I . . . I . . ."

"I know." Rachel's voice was gentle. "When you were with him it was easier to forget about what's been going on with your mom and dad."

Casey nodded, squeezing her eyes shut.

"But you can't forget about it forever. Sometime soon, you're going to have to deal with it."

"I know," Casey said. But she didn't know, didn't want to know, what "dealing with it" might mean. She looked up at Rachel suddenly. "Do you think I'll ever see Dad again?"

Rachel frowned and something akin to anger darkened her eyes as she remembered the pain Russell had caused her lovely, good-natured Sunny, marring not only the surface of her skin, but her spirits as well. "I don't know," she replied carefully, trying to keep the bitterness out of her usually lilting voice. "We only hear from him through the lawyers."

"Well, I want to see him," Casey said, with a fierceness that she hadn't known she felt. "If I could just talk to him, maybe I could get him to explain that he really didn't mean it all those times he . . . all those things he did to Mom. Then we could go back to West Hartford and things would be okay again."

Sunny appeared in the doorway, tying her thick, shoulder-length hair back with a pale blue ribbon. "Things are not going to be okay again, Casey, if we go back to West Hartford." Her voice sounded tired but determined. "I'm sorry about the glass, Mom. I'll replace it tomorrow." Rachel nodded. "Come on, Casey, let's go for our walk now."

"But it's so hot out. Can't we go after supper when it's cooler?"

"Tonight is the first *Godspell* rehearsal," Sunny replied. "So it's now or never."

Casey would have opted for never, but their beach walks had turned into a weekly event. Even in the winter, they had gone out and found new beaches to explore. The multitude of sea glass, stones, shells, and driftwood scattered through the house attested to their weekly ventures, as well as to Grandma Rachel's collections over the years.

Casey stood up and emptied her cereal dish in the sink, watching the soggy mass filter down the drain. "Okay Mom," she said with quiet resignation. "Let's go."

CHAPTER 3

They drove in silence to nearby Eastbrook Beach. Casey and Sunny left their shoes in the car and made their way through the blankets and sunbathers to the edge of the chilled salt water, which swirled in foaming rhythm around their toes like playful kittens. Their silence was punctuated by the laughter of little children splashing in the waves, and muted music pouring from speakers all along the beach behind them.

Casey was certain that Sunny was going to talk about what happened the night before and would demand an explanation of why she insisted on seeing Eric when she had promised not to.

But Sunny was walking silently, leading them away from the crowded beach and toward the jetty. Once in a while, she bent over to examine a shell or piece of colored sea glass, occasionally brushing off the sand and putting the treasure in her pocket.

Casey was glad for the silence. It was easier to bear than the reminder that she had caused her mother even more pain.

They walked for several more minutes until the jetty was only several yards away. Suddenly, Sunny stopped and shaded her eyes from the sun. "They finally set the court date for the divorce," she said.

Casey tried to match her mother's calm tone, but her stomach began sinking further and further to the ground. "Okay." She swallowed hard. "When?"

"August twentieth."

Casey tensed. "Can't it . . . can't it wait a little longer?"

"Wait? Why would I want to *wait*?" Sunny began to walk again, headed for the ragged jetty of huge, dark rocks.

Casey followed her, chewing a broken fingernail while she watched her mother climb onto one of the lower rocks. She shrugged. "I don't know. If we give him enough time, maybe Dad will decide he's sorry and make it up to you."

"I know you really want that, but I don't believe it's possible anymore," Sunny said. She sat on the rock facing Casey, and patted the space beside her.

Casey looked away. Out on the horizon several sailboats drifted lazily. She wished she were out there drifting too. Away from this. Carefully she climbed up next to her mother.

"We're not going back, Casey. You've got to get used to that."

"But . . ."

"He wasn't good to us, sweetie. You know that."

"He was always good to *me*," she replied stubbornly,

lifting her heavy hair off of her neck and twisting it over her shoulder.

Sunny looked at her daughter incredulously. "No, he wasn't. Don't you remember our last night with him?"

Casey chewed on her broken nail again. How could she forget? It had been her mother's birthday, October fourteenth, and her father had not come home for the special dinner Casey had made. A chill ran up Casey's neck as she recalled going to bed that night but not being able to sleep. When her father had finally come home around midnight, she was strumming her guitar and could hear his coarse voice berating Sunny even over the music and even though her bedroom door was closed, as was her parents'. Then other violent sounds had silenced her guitar. She had heard his belligerent slapping and her mother's screams as she begged him to stop.

Casey had opened her bedroom door, trembling. Every time this had happened, she'd vowed that next time she would do something. Call the police. Phone a neighbor. Rush in and beg her father to stop. Something.

Yet every time that the "next time" came, she froze with fear, hoping against hope that it would be over soon. She knew the pattern. After the attack was over, he would go into their private bathroom and take a long shower. When he came out, there would be silence. And it was never mentioned again.

But this time had been different. Instead of going straight to the shower, her father had opened their bedroom door. "And it's too damned late to be playing that idiotic guitar," he yelled as he strode toward Casey's room. Then he had seen her standing in her doorway, clutching the door, a frozen figure wrapped in her favorite fluffy purple robe. For an instant he had frozen too, as if for the first time realizing that his daughter knew what he did to her mother behind those closed doors. Then, in continued rage, perhaps at himself, he picked up the closest object, a solid gray marble ashtray from the phone table in the hall, and threw it straight at Casey.

Two things happened at once. Casey quickly dodged out of the ashtray's path and watched as it smashed into her bureau, shattering her favorite crystalline music box into a million tiny pieces. And Sunny, bruised and bleeding, her nightgown torn, screamed at her to go back in her room and lock the door.

Casey had done so, crying and trembling. Then she sank to the floor, her back against the door. She had sat like that the entire night—a fearful, vulnerable, unarmed guard.

In the morning, after Russell left for work, Sunny had told her to pack her two suitcases because they were going to Grandma Rachel's house in Woodfield. There were dark, splotchy bruises on Sunny's arms and neck. One eye was completely swollen shut, the color of shiny eggplant.

Although Woodfield was only an hour from West Hartford, it had seemed like the longest drive of their lives. From time to time, Sunny had cried openly, but Casey had sat like a mannequin, willing herself into a steely numbness so she could be strong for her mother.

All of that seemed a long time ago as she sat beside her mother now on a sea-sprayed rock, looking out at the ocean. A lot had happened since then. Sunny had gotten a job as a teacher's aide in a special education class in New Haven, about ten minutes away. Casey had met Eric in December at Woodfield High. He was older, a drop-out, but hung around the parking lot during lunch and after school. She had found relief and comfort in his arms.

Sunny was finding relief and comfort at Grace Church and in counseling sessions with Peter Wright, the young minister there. She seemed a lot happier and more confident lately. She'd had no bruises for a long time. Her skin was golden and smooth, except for the long shiny scar on her left forearm which served as a constant, ugly reminder of all they had been through.

Casey looked at her mother. She wasn't willing to let go of her father just yet. "I don't think he really meant to hurt me when he threw that ashtray. He was just angry. Besides, he knew I'd duck out of the way before it hit me."

"Being angry doesn't justify hurting people," Sunny replied, jumping off the rock and turning to face her daughter, hands on her hips.

"But he never hurt me. Only you."

"Your father never hurt you physically. But he did hurt you in ways you don't understand yet. No child should have to witness their mother being hurt like that for so many years."

Casey joined her mother in the wet sand. She picked up a small jagged rock and threw it far, far out into the ocean. She shook her head, her voice insistent. "We had lots of good times, too. Don't you ever remember the *good* times?"

"Of course I remember how good it was at the beginning." Sunny bit her lower lip.

"Dad wasn't always mean. We went to Yankee Stadium lots of times when I was little. He was such a baseball fanatic. That's why he named me Casey, remember? He took us to museums and the ballet and musicals and the circus. He was lots of fun then. When I was little. When he wasn't working so much." Casey threw another stone with all her might and watched with satisfaction as it plunged into the distant water.

"I remember those times too, Hon," Sunny said, gazing out over the water, shading her eyes. "But those weren't the only times. Russ changed after we were married for ten years. You were seven when it started. I don't know what made him hurt me like that. Maybe I'll never know. But I do know that I couldn't let it go on. And watching him throw that ashtray at you was the last straw. I guess I wasn't strong enough to protect myself all those years, but I found the strength within me to protect you."

Casey balled her hands into fists and started at her mother belligerently. "Am I supposed to thank you or something?"

Sunny frowned, then sighed. "No, Casey. I don't expect you to thank me."

"Well, good. Because I miss him. He used to sing with me when I'd play the guitar, remember? He'd buy the sheet music to every musical we went to, and then we'd spend hours learning the words and I'd spend hours practicing the chords." Casey's voice dropped to a whisper, a lump in her throat obstructing the full impact of her words. "I loved singing with him. I still miss him."

"I know you do," Sunny responded gently, putting her arm around Casey. They walked this way along the water's edge for a while. "But you can't tell me you miss the bad times."

Casey dragged her feet in the sand. She had to admit it was a relief not to worry so much about her mother. To be freed from the helplessness she had continually felt. Not to be faced with her mom's fresh bruises the mornings after. Never again to be a prisoner of the violent silence which had so often infiltrated their house.

"I hated it when he hurt you like that," she admitted fiercely, brushing back her bangs which were damp with humidity. "I hated it."

Sunny tightened her arm around Casey's shoulders. "I hated it too." They walked in close silence back to the car. Once inside, Sunny started the car and the soothing cool air streamed out of the open vents. She turned toward her daughter. "Do you think you can tell the judge at the divorce hearing how much you hated it when your dad hit me?"

Casey immediately began chewing another hangnail. "Why do *I* have to tell the judge *anything*?"

"Our lawyer says we have a better chance of getting a good settlement if you testify. And maybe the judge will be able to make your dad go into a treatment program. If he gets the right kind of help, they'll lift the restraining order, and then he could visit you."

"Was this your lawyer's idea, or yours?"

Sunny gripped the steering wheel. "I told my lawyer not to use you as a witness unless he absolutely had to. But there are no other witnesses. It was always just the three of us. We never had friends over to the house and I didn't go out much." Casey nodded. She remembered. She'd never been able to bring friends home, either.

"Honey, if there was anything I could do to keep you out of all this, I would. But I don't see any other way. You are the only one who saw what he did to me."

Casey leaned her head wearily against the headrest. She had barely escaped appearing before the judge for her arrest the night before. Now there was going to be another judge, for another reason. She would have preferred to take the consequences for the arrest; it would have been much easier.

"I don't have much of a choice, Mom, do I?" she asked quietly.

"You don't have to do this, Casey. I told my lawyer it would have to be your decision."

Casey heard the pain in her mother's voice. What would it be like to spend all those years with a man whose touch was brutal and unloving? She looked out the window. "It's okay, Mom," she said quietly, half hoping her words would be carried away on the hot summer wind. "I'll do it."

CHAPTER 4

When Casey stepped inside the cool basement of Grace Episcopal Church that evening, the first thing she noticed was the bright-yellow upright piano by the stage. The second thing she noticed was the small group of teenagers standing around it. They were laughing at something the petite woman at the piano was saying.

Casey's heart sank. She had hoped she'd be the first to arrive. She hated, absolutely hated, walking into a group of people who had already established friendships. It happened to her when she'd moved to West Hartford. It happened to her at Woodfield High. And now it was happening again.

But she had no other choice. Even if she stayed by the door, they would notice her eventually. She walked slowly toward them, her heart pounding.

The woman at the piano had begun playing a lively tune, but she stopped when she noticed Casey. Her movements were lively, her voice as light and airy as her short, feathery hair. "Hi there!" She raised a slender hand in

greeting. Casey noticed it was adorned with many colorful rings and bracelets. "I'm Marianne, Peter's wife. He
bribed me into being the accompanist for *Godspell*. Actually, I'm a brilliant—" she winked at the others, "—com-
poser and pianist for the New England Symphony up in
Hartford." She paused and studied the tall red-haired girl
in front of her. "You must be Casey."

"Yes . . . Casey Donovan. Hi." She glanced nervously
at the strangers' faces around her and raised a hand in a
half wave.

Marianne chatted on. "I was just telling everyone
about the time when Peter played the role of Jesus in
Godspell at Yale Divinity School. It was *many* years ago,
I might add." She shook her head with laughter and her
long, silver earrings swayed back and forth. "Anyway, at
the beginning of the play, John the Baptist is supposed
to wash Jesus's feet. And everything would have been fine
except Peter forgot to take his socks off before he came onstage! No one noticed until the guy who played John bent
over to wipe Peter's feet with the sponge. They both realized the problem at the same time and burst into laughter.
Right there in front of the audience."

A stocky boy with thin brown hair pinched his nose
with two fingers and poked the slim boy beside him.
"Ugh! No way am I taking your socks off, Chris!"

"Listen, Neil," said Chris, whose deep voice seemed a
surprise, coming out of such a slight body. "I just might
decide to wear my grandfather's old lace-up army boots.

Then you'll have more to do than just remove my socks!"

The girl standing beside Casey laughed along with the rest, then said to her, "Don't mind those two, they're really best friends. My name's Suzanne," she added with a smile.

"And I'm Megan," said the tall, confident-looking girl on the other side of the piano. She had long, curly dark hair.

The younger girl next to Megan spoke softly, almost in a whisper. "I'm Kate." She wore thick, tortoise shell glasses on her wide face which was framed with short brown hair.

Casey's voice held uncertainty. "I think I've seen some of you around school."

"Right!" said Suzanne, in sudden recognition. "You were in my last period study hall."

"Mr. Fitchman?"

"Yeah!" Suzanne faked a scowl. "Some grouch, huh?"

Casey forgot her nervousness and giggled. "We used to say that maybe he ought to turn his bed around since he always seemed to get up on the wrong side of it."

Marianne chuckled at this. "Well, Casey, I see you'll fit right in with this bunch! We're just waiting for Jeff and Abby. And Peter had to make a few hospital calls after supper. He should be here any minute. We were going over the first song from *Godspell*, 'Prepare Ye the Way of The Lord.' John the Baptist sings this as he's baptizing you, the disciples. Then Jesus appears and insists that John baptize him as well. Neil will begin singing this as a solo since he's John the Baptist, but you'll all sing this as you come onstage."

"And it's *really* hard," Neil said to Casey with a fake grimace. "Lots of words to memorize."

"Seven, to be exact," interrupted Marianne. "Think you guys can handle it?"

They all laughed. "My parents took me to see this once when I was nine or ten," Suzanne said. "And I think the cast entered from the back of the auditorium. Is that right?"

Marianne nodded. "You enter by dancing up the aisles, shaking hands with the people in the audience. It's supposed to have the feeling of a party."

"Yeah, but this is about the Gospel," said Megan with a frown. "I thought it was supposed to be serious."

"It is serious," answered Marianne, resting her fingers lightly on the keyboard. "But Jesus didn't mean for us to be serious all the time. Most of the script gives you a chance to play while learning the things Jesus taught, and to entertain the audience while you're teaching them. You'll be acting out a lot of Jesus's parables, and there are lots of opportunities for hamming it up—"

"Which shouldn't be a problem for *this* group, now should it?" asked Peter as he appeared on the stage and nimbly jumped off it, walking toward the group. He wore black pants and shirt with a white clerical collar.

Laying some folders on top of the piano, he leaned over and kissed Marianne lightly on the cheek.

"So how is everyone tonight?" Peter asked.

"Great!" We've already memorized the first song!" announced Neil with a grin.

"And we also heard the infamous Sock Story," said Megan, fishing around in her purse, then clipping a crisp white barrette with trailing slender ribbons into her dark wavy hair.

Peter groaned. "Oh no, not that!" he said to Marianne in mock embarrassment. "You didn't tell them that one!"

She held up her hands in surrender. "They made me do it, I swear."

"Yeah, sure!" Peter said, still laughing. He put his hand on Casey's shoulder. "I'm glad you made it, Casey," he said. "What do you think so far? Is this group nuts or what?" She noticed for the first time that his voice held the slightest warmth of a southern accent.

She smiled and drummed her fingers nervously on the edge of the piano, briefly wondering why it was bright yellow. Everyone was looking at her, expectantly. "It's okay," she answered quietly.

"Hey," said Chris suddenly. "You must be a good singer or Peter wouldn't have asked you to join us. Ever done a musical like this before?"

Casey felt her cheeks redden. She realized, thankfully, that Peter hadn't told them exactly why she was here. She glanced at him. He was smiling at her, his dark brown eyes suggesting that this was a safe place.

"I . . . I've never done a musical. But I like to sing. My mother and grandmother go to church here but I . . . haven't yet. My parents used to take me to the theater before they . . . I mean, when I was younger. My dad used to

35

buy me the scores and I'd learn to play them on the guitar, and we'd sing all the songs together, over and over. Mom said they had to keep taking me to new musicals so she could hear some different music around the house."

"Then why haven't you joined the chorus at school?" asked Megan, winding a long, dark curl around her forefinger. "We sure could use some more voices."

"I don't know," said Casey uneasily, although she knew perfectly well why. Eric had wanted her to spend all of her free time with him.

"Maybe you can join in the fall," said Chris hopefully.

"Maybe," she murmured, her gaze riveted to the piano.

"Hey!" said Suzanne. "I've got a great idea! You could do the other solo. Megan's doing one and so is Abby. They wanted Kate or me to do the other one, but—"

"But I am *not* a singer," finished Kate.

"And I would love to be a singer, but God left the beautiful singing voice out when He created me," added Suzanne.

Casey shook her head, looking from one friendly face to another.

"Isn't there a song where someone is supposed to be playing guitar in the background?" asked Suzanne. "That would be perfect for Casey!"

"*Day by Day* is sometimes sung by two people instead of one," said Marianne, reaching quickly for one of the three-ring binders that lay on the piano. She flipped through the pages of the script. "It could very easily be done with one person playing guitar and the other singing harmony."

"Wait a minute," said Casey timidly. "I haven't picked up the guitar since I moved here last Fall. I'm not sure I—"

Neil interrupted hopefully. "Maybe it's like riding a bike. Once you learn, you never forget?"

Casey's stomach was beginning to churn. "I don't know," she said. "I don't even know the song. I don't want to ruin your show, after all."

"What do you mean, *your* show?" asked Peter. "This is *our* show, and you're an important part of it."

"That's right, Casey," said Marianne. "Besides, you'll hear the song Thursday night when we see *Godspell* over at Yale. You don't have to decide anything right now."

"Okay," said Casey hesitantly, but she had already decided. Her guitar was going to stay under her bed.

The door in the back of the room suddenly burst open and everyone looked around to see who it was.

"Hi everyone!" called a slender girl with loose, frizzy blond hair as she raced across the room. "Sorry I'm late," she added breathlessly, flinging a bright red purse onto the stage and joining her friends at the piano.

"No problem, Abby," said Neil casually. "We were just discussing who to give your solo to."

"Very funny, Neil." Abby put her pale hands around his wide throat and pretended to choke him as everyone laughed, then leaned her elbows on the piano and surveyed the group. "I really am sorry I'm late, okay? My mom was on the phone with one of her friends, so of course we didn't eat dinner until late and—"

"I don't have a good excuse," said a good-looking, dark-haired boy who had arrived quietly in the midst of Abby's noisy entrance. "I'm just late."

"Oh, Jeff, you're always late!" exclaimed Megan good naturedly. With their dark wavy hair and light blue eyes, they looked enough alike to be brother and sister. "If you ever got anywhere on time, we'd probably all think our phones were wrong!"

"Yeah, yeah. Thanks a lot," Jeff said, the crease lines in his forehead smoothing out as he grinned.

"Well," said Peter. "Now that everyone is *finally* here." They all laughed. "We'd better get started. Jeff and Abby, this is Casey. She's going to join us for *Godspell*."

"Hey, nice to meet you," said Jeff, his voice and eyes warm and welcoming.

"Same here," Casey managed to say. She felt something tugging at her heart. He had to be the best-looking guy she'd ever met, but there was something else about him, something in his eyes that went deeper than a surface attraction.

CHAPTER 5

"First of all," said Peter after they had arranged some folding chairs in a circle beside the stage. "It's important that you have some idea of what *Godspell* is all about. Suzanne, I know you've seen it. Do you remember anything about it?"

Suzanne's vivid smile lit up her hazel eyes. "Sure. It's a musical about the ministry of Jesus. It's based on the Gospel of Matthew, I think, right? So it starts when John the Baptist baptizes Jesus and ends when Jesus dies on the cross."

"Not a very happy ending," said Megan, smoothing her hair back and crossing her legs.

"That depends on how you look at it," answered Peter. "We all know that God raised Jesus from the dead after three days. *That's* the happy ending."

Marianne spoke up. "As a matter of fact, we've seen the play done where they add a scene to the end of the script so Jesus comes back to life right on stage. It's pretty powerful stuff."

"Could *we* do it that way?" asked Abby, leaning forward, her hair covering her eyes. She popped a piece of gum in her mouth and tucked the wrapper in her purse.

"Depends on the rest of the group. If everyone wants to, it's okay by me."

"Let's wait until we see it Thursday at Yale," said Chris, scratching at the acne on his wide forehead. "Then we'll know what we're talking about."

"Okay," said Abby. "I just thought since we're supposed to be teaching people about how wonderful God is, we should maybe include the Resurrection?"

The others were nodding and murmuring in agreement when Casey mumbled something under her breath.

"What did you say?" Peter asked kindly, turning toward her.

Casey's stomach lurched. She hadn't meant for anyone to hear her. "N . . . nothing."

"Come on, Casey," said Abby, who was sitting next to her. "Don't be shy, okay? If you've got something to say, this is the place to say it."

Casey shifted in her chair and looked around at the friendly faces. *Okay. If they want to hear it, they will.* "I said I don't think God is so wonderful. I don't believe in Him." She crossed her arms on her stomach and waited, aware of the bristling curiosity around her.

Peter sat relaxed, his legs stretched out in front of him, hands resting on his thighs. "That's all right, Casey," he said gently. "You don't have to believe in God to be in

Godspell. But you really ought to believe in *something* . . . Maybe yourself?"

Casey thought for a moment, then quickly shook her head, eyes fixed on the floor.

"How about love?" asked Marianne.

"It depends what kind. I love my mom. I love the beach, I guess. I love music."

"All right then!" exclaimed Peter, sitting upright in his chair. *Godspell's* all about expressing our feelings and the stories of Jesus through music. All you need to do is believe in the power of the music to tell the story. Can you do that?"

Casey shrugged, fearful of what the others were thinking about her. "I guess so," she mumbled, looking down. "Sorry about interrupting the discussion."

"You didn't interrupt anything," replied Peter. "You just became a part of it."

"He's right," said Jeff. "Most of us have been coming here for a while and if there's one thing we've learned, it's okay to say what's on our minds. At least we have a place where we can do that here. I can't say what I want to at home or I get grounded for weeks."

"Thanks." Casey studied her ragged fingernails, remembering countless arguments with her mother about Eric. "I know what you mean."

"Well, as long as we're saying what's on our minds," Abby said brightly, still chewing her gum. "I want to know what kind of costumes we're going to wear for this production. I mean, are we all going to wear robes and sandals like Jesus did or what?"

Marianne leaned forward in her seat and eagerly rubbed her palms together, her bracelets making a light, silvery sound. "You're going to love this. Nobody wears robes and sandals. Everyone gets to create their own costume!"

"What do you mean?" asked Kate, quietly. She pushed her glasses back with a short finger.

Marianne continued. "The idea is to wear colorful clothes with a childlike quality. Jesus tells us that it's important to become like little children in order to enter the Kingdom of Heaven. The characters in this play have many childlike qualities and it's hard to project childlikeness to the audience if you're wearing long robes and sandals."

"You'll see what Marianne means when you see *Godspell* this week," said Peter. "Jesus usually wears a Superman shirt, suspenders and bright pants."

"And bare feet," added Neil, lightly punching Chris. "Don't forget the bare feet!"

"Right, right. And I'm sure Peter has a Superman T-shirt he can loan you, Chris," said Jeff. "He seems to have one to suit every other occasion!"

Peter chuckled good naturedly. "As a matter of fact, I do have a Superman shirt just like that."

When the laughter died down, Peter went on. "The idea for the costumes is to look casual and playful.

"Very thrown-together," added Marianne.

"It's like a come-as-you-are party," Peter said. Jesus invites us to come to Him as we are."

"I get it!" said Suzanne, her delicate features animated. "I could wear my dad's pajama bottoms and my brother's letter sweater, with a big straw hat that has fresh flowers woven into it."

"That's the idea. We'll help you if you want, but try to come up with a costume that expresses who you are or who you want to be."

"You'll get some more ideas Thursday night," Marianne said. "And you won't need to wear it until the end of August, so you've got lots of time."

"Any other questions?" Peter asked. They shook their heads. "Okay, then. There's one more thing I want us to do tonight. Remember how we said Jesus asks us to be childlike?"

"Not child-ish," Marianne pointed out.

"That's right. There's a difference. Let's think of some of the qualities little children have that we tend to lose as we get older. Qualities that Jesus might want us to have. Any ideas?"

"Well," Suzanne began, playing with the bright turquoise ring on her right middle finger. "My little sister Penny is very trusting. I mean, if you tell her something, she just believes that it's true."

"And how about you? Now that you're older, have you lost that ability to trust?"

"It's harder, but usually I'm pretty trusting."

Neil spoke seriously for a change. "I agree. Little kids are more trusting than I am. It's hard to trust someone who never follows through on what they promise. After people break their promises to you enough times, it's not safe to trust them."

Abby nodded. "I know what you mean, Neil, but I don't seem to have a hard time trusting people. It's God I have a hard time with, know what I mean?" She chewed her gum more vigorously.

Surprised, Casey looked over at her.

Abby smoothed out the material of her jeans. "Children trust God because they're told that's what they're supposed to do," she went on, her voice still strong. "But sometimes when you get older, things happen . . ." She stopped abruptly and stared blankly across the hall.

"And?" questioned Peter, raising his right eyebrow with interest.

Abby refocused on the group, and put her feet on her chair, encircling her knees with her arms. "And sometimes you just have to wonder why God lets certain things happen, okay? I believe in God. I just don't understand. . . . How does He fit into my life, right here and now?"

"Good question," said Peter. "Anyone have any answers?"

"Darn, Peter, we thought *you* had all the answers!" replied Neil.

Peter hesitated. "Sometimes I talk too much. I think I'll see what others have to say this time."

"Well," said Megan. "I think maybe God fits into our

lives in different ways at different times."

Jeff shoved his hands in his pockets. "Right, right. And we have to ask Him why certain things happen—"

"And then what, just wait for the answers?" Abby's voice was thin and brittle, as though it might break into a thousand jagged pieces. She abruptly stood, walked to the wastebasket near the piano and threw her gum into it.

Jeff looked startled. He cleared his throat, then looked doubtfully at Peter.

"Waiting is the hardest part, Abby," Peter finally said. "Listening. Waiting. Sometimes it takes a long time before we understand the good that God can bring out of what seemed like a disaster, or to understand where God was when we were going through a hard time."

Abby's catlike green eyes glistened with tears, but she sat down again. "Well, sometimes I get tired of waiting, okay?" She took in a deep breath. "I watched my big brother *drown*. I tried to save him, but I couldn't." Her voice trembled as she looked around the group. "I loved Preston. He was going to be an actor. That's why I like doing all these plays and stuff. It's a part of him I can keep alive somehow, know what I mean? But . . ." She squeezed her eyes shut for a moment. "I know he's never coming back." Her voice rose. "And I don't see how God was there, when he . . . when he drowned. If God was *there*, he would have kept Preston *alive*." She angrily shook her head and brought her knees close to her chest, resting her feet on her chair, clenching her small body tightly together.

Suzanne immediately reached over Casey's lap to touch Abby's arm. "I'm sorry. I didn't know."

Abby looked up. "It was three years ago, before we moved here. I haven't been able to talk about it much. My parents have paid for all kinds of therapy, but it hasn't helped." A few tears trickled down her cheek and she angrily brushed them away.

"It must have been awful, Abby," said Peter. "I know how it feels. I've watched lots of people die."

"I don't think I could ever do that again," Abby said, her voice clogged with tears. "How do you stand it?"

"Well, something wonderful usually happens right before a person dies. Even if they've been unconscious for a long time. They open their eyes and you can tell they're seeing again, but they're not seeing you or what's around them. Their face lights up and sometimes they smile. Sometimes they say something, but whatever they're looking at puts them at perfect peace before they close their eyes again." He looked at Abby. "I can see that peace on their faces. That's what makes it easier for me to stand it."

"Do you think they see God right before they die?" Kate spoke softly, in wonder.

"I'm sure of it. Nothing else could take away all that pain and sadness, and replace it with such perfect peace."

Casey's heart lifted and she relaxed in spite of herself. She had always wondered about death, about what would happen if her father had actually killed her mother one of those times he was so angry. She hadn't known how she would bear it. Now it seemed there was some hope.

"Did something like that happen with Preston?" Megan was asking Abby.

Abby put her feet back on the floor and pressed her palms together, thinking back. A smile began to dawn on her tear-stained face. "Yes, yes, it did," she began slowly. "I haven't thought about this part in a long time, but . . . I could tell the exact moment he died because right before, he opened his eyes and looked at me, right at me. And he smiled." Her own smile got brighter. "I could tell he could see me, but it was more like he was seeing everything about me, everything that was going to happen to me in the future and everything that had happened to me in the past. I never knew how to explain it before now, you know?"

Casey caught her breath. Neil gave a low whistle. Megan said "Wow!" softly and in wonder.

"Did he say anything to you?" Chris asked.

Abby shook her head. "He didn't have to. He was looking right at me and smiling so . . . peacefully. I was crying too much to really pay much attention at the time. But I remember now. . . . He nodded, like he was approving of everything that he saw. And he squeezed my hand very hard, like he was passing something on to me, and then he closed his eyes and . . . just stopped breathing." She breathed deeply for a moment, then smiled. "I forgot most of that until just now." She pushed some strands of her frizzy blond hair off her forehead. "Preston left so peacefully, just like you said, Peter. Maybe God . . . maybe God really was there after all? Her voice trailed off in wonder, still questioning.

"Oh yes," said Peter gently. "I'm sure He was there."

Abby slowly moved her head and studied the group for a moment. "Yes," she said simply. "Yes. Thank you. Thank you all for . . . for listening to me and everything."

"That's why we're here, Abby," said Peter. "You okay now?"

Abby nodded.

"All right then, we all agreed that one childlike trait is trust. How about some more? Chris?"

"Who me?"

"Yes, you! You have four younger brothers and sisters. Surely you must have noticed something about them that's different from adults."

"Well, now that you mention it, they do seem *louder* than most grown-ups, especially when they're all in the same room!"

"Okay, I asked for that one!" Peter replied, grinning. "Anything besides volume?"

"Well, said Chris. "Little kids have more fun than adults. I mean, they're always playing, getting dirty, having a good time. The older you get, the more responsibility you have, and the less time there is to have fun."

"But that doesn't *have* to be true," Kate said carefully.

"What do you mean?" asked Marianne.

"Like, I'm really serious about studying and school

and stuff. I have lots of responsibility at home with Mom working all day, and Molly being in so many activities in Junior High. But that doesn't mean that there's any less time to have fun than when I was little. It just means that . . . I don't know . . . I guess I'm so used to being serious that half the time it never occurs to me to have fun anymore."

Marianne smiled at Kate. "I know what you mean. Especially an old, married couple like us! We can get so wrapped up in our jobs and responsibilities that we forget to have fun. Peter and I try to do something fun together every week. Even if it's just watching an old "Will & Grace" episode on TV together. Laughter is important, but you have to sometimes *make* time for it."

Casey frowned. There hadn't been much laughter when Eric was around. Or her father, either.

"But what if something really sad is going on in your life?" asked Chris. "How can God expect you to be having fun then? You know, my grandfather's really sick. And lately it doesn't seem like there's very much to laugh about."

"Well, there's a time and place for everything," Peter said after some deliberation. "When you're sad, it would be a lie to go out and pretend to be happy. You have to be honest enough with yourself to know when to cry and when to laugh."

"Isn't there something in the Old Testament about that?" asked Suzanne. "A time to be born and a time to die, a time to weep and a time to laugh . . . ?"

"Yes," said Marianne. "It's from Ecclesiastes. A friend

of ours read it at our wedding. "A time to break down and a time to build up; a time to mourn and a time to dance; a time to seek and a time to lose . . . It goes on and on."

Casey swallowed hard. Were those words really in the Bible? Was it really possible that it was okay for her not to believe in God and not to feel like dancing because she was so confused inside? And if she didn't believe in God, then why did His words seem to reach so deep within her?

Marianne glanced at her watch. "Well, I see we've gotten way off track here, Peter. It's almost time to go. Isn't there something you want them to do for next time?"

"You're giving us *homework*?" exclaimed Neil and Chris in unison.

Megan made a face and tossed her hair over her shoulder. "Come on Peter, give us a break. We just got out of school two weeks ago!"

"This really isn't too bad." He picked up a folder from the piano. "You can have fun with this one, and you don't need to write anything down. Just think about it." He handed a piece of paper to each of them.

"It's a drawing of some kids at a playground," Abby said. "What do you want us to do with it?"

"Just look at the different children in the picture and decide which one you most identify with and why. We'll talk about it next Sunday." Peter stood and laid the folder on his chair.

"That's it?" Megan asked. "I don't get it."

"Yeah," added Jeff. "What does this have to do with

Godspell?"

Peter gestured for them to stand up. "We're trying to be more childlike in our *Godspell* roles, right?"

Jeff nodded.

"Well, this will help you get in touch with your own specific childlike qualities."

"And when you start to develop your character for the play, you can use what you learn from this picture," said Marianne. "Don't worry about it. See what you can discover about yourself between now and next Sunday."

"Okay," said Jeff with a shrug. "If you say so."

"Any more questions?" No one answered. "Then let's say the Lord's Prayer and we can all go home."

The others moved in closer together, putting their arms around each other in the circle. For a moment, Casey froze. This was obviously their traditional way of ending Youth Group meetings. Surely they didn't expect her to join them. But suddenly Abby's and Suzanne's arms were around her shoulders, pulling her into the circle. Slowly, she lifted her arms around theirs.

The others closed their eyes, bowed their heads and began to pray softly. Casey was silent, unwilling to say words she didn't believe. Instead, she studied each person in the circle. Suzanne's caramel colored hair fell around her delicate face but did not hide the radiant smile that transformed her plain features.

"Hallowed be thy name . . ." Peter was smiling also, but it was the smile of a friend telling another friend a won-

derful secret.

"Thy kingdom come, thy will be done . . ." Neil's chubby round face was unusually still and serious. Chris seemed serious also, his angular face pale and lovely in spite of the acne. Casey shivered. He almost reminded her of Jesus, the way his head was bowed, the intense look of concentration on his face.

"On earth as it is in heaven . . ." The colored ribbons in Megan's dark hair fell across her cheekbones. Her lips were moving silently, and her face was still.

"Give us this day our daily bread . . ." Marianne's light brown eyes were open, and her gaze was fixed in the middle of the circle.

"And forgive us our trespasses . . ." Kate's eyes were squeezed shut and her lips moved with intense concentration.

"As we forgive those who trespass against us . . ." Jeff's thick dark hair fell in his eyes, which were closed. He wasn't smiling, but there was a look of peace and relief on his face that Casey hadn't seen there before.

"Lead us not into temptation, but deliver us from evil." Abby was staring at her feet. Her blond hair obscured most of her face, but Casey could see that she was saying the words with a new look of wonder, as though she'd never heard the prayer before.

"For thine is the kingdom and the power and the glory . . ." Casey realized that Peter was looking at her. She panicked, but he just winked at her and grinned. Casey relaxed and joined in the ending.

"Forever and ever. Amen." Suzanne and Abby squeezed her shoulders in the brief group hug that followed.

"We'll see you in the parking lot Thursday night at 5:30 to leave for Yale, okay?" Peter called out as everyone headed for the door.

Casey folded the picture of the children into a tiny square and put it in her jeans pocket as she walked silently to the exit, ahead of the others. Her mind was spinning with all the feelings that had paraded through her in the last few hours. Fear. Acceptance. Peace. Confusion.

Suzanne caught up with her as she reached the door. "I'm really glad you came tonight, Casey."

"Thanks." Some of Casey's confusion melted away as they stepped together into the humid night air.

Suzanne nodded at the small blue car that was waiting at the curb. "Is that your mom?"

"Yeah, I'd better go."

"See you Thursday, okay?" Suzanne called from the sidewalk.

"Okay. Bye."

Casey got into the car and looked over at her mother.

"Well?" Sunny asked cautiously, steeling herself for any outburst that might occur. "How did it go?"

Casey fastened her seatbelt and looked back at the church for a moment as they pulled away from the curb. "Not as bad as I thought it would," she replied, surprised to find that it was true.

CHAPTER 6

Later that week, Casey sat on the front porch steps of her grandmother's old house, the drawing of the children in her hands. She stared at it intently.

There were eight children in the picture. Two of them were on a seesaw: one was up in the air and the other was on the ground. One child was beginning to climb a gigantic tree; another was already in the topmost branches. A child was sitting on the ground, simply watching the activity around him. There was a happy child on a swing high in the air. The last two children were playing on a slide. One was at the bottom of the ladder, with her foot on the first rung. The other was at the top, clutching the sides in fear.

Casey studied the drawing, then sighed. She had no idea which might represent her. She'd been so busy lately trying to act like an adult. Concentrating on childhood now was proving to be difficult.

Grandma Rachel came out of the house, letting the green, wooden screen door bang shut behind her. She plopped into one of the white wicker porch chairs and fanned herself with a magazine. "What are you looking at?"

Casey stood up, stretched, and sat next to Rachel in a faded blue rocking chair. She showed her the picture and explained the assignment. Rachel set the magazine down and squinted at the drawing. "Yep, this seems like something Peter would think up! So, which child seems the most like you?"

Casey shook her head. "I just don't know. What do you think?"

"Doesn't matter what I think, dear. You'll have to figure that out for yourself. But I will tell you which one reminds me of me."

"Really?"

Grandma Rachel pointed to the boy halfway up the tree. "I was always doing things when I was young. Climbing trees, riding bikes, building tree forts. You name it, I did it. The bigger the tree and the steeper the hill, the better I liked it! I never really thought about if it was dangerous or scary or even if it was impossible. I just did it!"

Casey looked at her grandmother, trying hard to imagine her as a daring tomboy. Sunny joined them, setting a glass pitcher of lemonade and a tray of mugs on the small wooden table between the chairs. "What's this?" she asked as she settled herself into the flowered porch swing across from them.

Casey explained the assignment as Grandma Rachel poured the lemonade. "So which child are you, Mom?"

Sunny took the picture into her hands. "Hmmm . . ." she murmured. "That girl there on top of the slide . . . she looks like she doesn't quite want to let go."

"Did you get scared when you were a girl?" Casey asked softly, suddenly curious. She'd never thought about her mother being a child. She sipped the sweet lemonade from a tall, frosted mug and studied Sunny curiously.

Sunny tucked a leg under her on the swing. "Not as scared as I am right now." She sighed and looked into the lemonade as if it could comfort her in some way. She bit her lower lip in childlike vulnerability.

Casey didn't know what to say. She took the paper from her mother's hands and looked again at the child on top of the slide, caught somewhere between a beginning and an ending, between indecision and action. She looked as though she was relieved that the beginning was over but frightened of going any further. Casey looked up at her mother and sighed. Suddenly, she knew which child she identified with the most.

Light footsteps on the sidewalk and an upbeat, "Hi Casey, how's it going?" broke the solemn silence on the porch. It was Suzanne.

Casey brightened a little. "Hi!" Want some lemonade?"

"Sure." Suzanne sat down on the swing next to Sunny.

"It's good to see you again, dear," Grandma Rachel said. "I'll get another glass." She disappeared into the house and soon returned with a clean mug, the screen door banging both times. "Did you enjoy the show last night?" She poured the lemonade and handed it to Suzanne, the ice clinking against the glass.

"It was sooo good! I've seen *Godspell* before, but the Yale version was so much more . . . I don't know, alive somehow. Casey, what did you think?"

Casey crunched on an ice cube and nodded. "I really liked it." She couldn't find the right words to explain how the music, the characters, and the parables had touched her, but she imagined that Suzanne understood.

Rachel stood again and headed to the door. "Let's go inside, Sunny. The girls need some time to talk." She picked up the empty pitcher and glasses, and they entered the house, leaving the two girls alone.

Suzanne gazed dreamily across the porch. "I want to go there after high school."

"Go where?" Casey asked, confused.

"Yale."

"Really? Do you want to be an actor? Or a musician?"

"No," replied Suzanne seriously, eagerly. She sipped her lemonade. "A minister."

Casey stopped rocking. "You're kidding!"

Suzanne looked at Casey and shook her head. "No. That's really what I want to be . . . a minister."

"Like Peter?"

Suzanne laughed and the moment's intensity danced away. "Well, not exactly like Peter," she replied. "I'm not planning on buying a silly T-shirt for every day of the month!"

Casey laughed with her.

"Anyway . . ." Suzanne stretched her long slim legs in front of her and set the mug down. "I hope it's okay that I came over like this. I only live a few streets away."

"I'm glad you came. Perfect timing."

"What do you mean?"

"My mom looked at this drawing and found the child that reminded her of herself. I think it upset her."

Suzanne took the picture from Casey and studied it closely. "This was an interesting assignment, wasn't it?"

Casey shrugged. "I guess so. It was hard, that's for sure."

"Do you know which one is you?"

"I think so. You?"

Suzanne nodded. "I guess we'll talk about it tomorrow night. You ready for our first rehearsal?"

Casey tipped her mug and caught another piece of ice between her teeth. "Ready as I'll ever be, I guess."

"Have you thought any more about playing your guitar during *Day By Day*?"

Casey's stomach dropped and she felt her palms begin to sweat. "I really don't think I can do that."

"Did you try?" Suzanne asked gently.

Casey shook her head. "I haven't played since October, ever since we left my father. He used to sing. . . . He and I used to . . . " She faltered, searching for words. Suzanne waited patiently, eyes focused on Casey. "My father would sing with me while I played. I hardly ever played without him. The last few years were pretty hard. Then things got worse with him and my mom, and then . . . then we didn't sing together much toward the end. I don't know . . ."

Suzanne reached out and touched Casey's left hand which gripped the rocker so tightly that her knuckles were white. "It's okay. Megan can sing just as easily with the piano. Maybe you can just sing with her instead of playing the guitar."

Casey cleared her throat and tried to smile. "It's not that I don't want to. It's just that . . . I'm not sure if I'd be able to . . . without my Dad."

"Whatever you decide, it will be okay," Suzanne replied gently as she laid the picture on the table and slowly stood. "I've got to get back home now. Do you want to walk to rehearsal together tomorrow night?"

Casey nodded. "Sure. Thanks. See you tomorrow." She watched Suzanne's slender form until it had completely disappeared into the lengthening shadows. Then she walked over to the top wooden step and sat down on it, staring at the flickering street light.

Thoughts of Eric faded in and out with the glimmers of light. His presence in her life had brought a certain brightness, and she had imagined that his absence had doomed her to eternal shadows. But now another light was beginning to shimmer around her and some of the darkness was fading.

The streetlight stopped flickering and shone steadily in the dim summer sky.

✻

CHAPTER 7

"Grab a paintbrush!" called Peter as Casey and Suzanne walked into the church basement the next night. He was wearing a blue T-shirt with the words GET SERIOUS in large yellow letters. "We're painting the backdrop for the show. It's going to be a brick wall with graffiti all over it."

"And the graffiti is our names," called Neil, precariously balanced atop a ladder at the far end of the stage.

"The idea is to paint your name in a way that most expresses who you are. Not how you look on the outside, but who you are on the inside."

Suzanne dropped her purse on the piano and ran up the stairs to the stage. "I'm ready!" she announced, picking up a paintbrush and a jar of yellow paint and taking it to an area of the backdrop that was not yet filled. She immediately swept the outline of a shining, fluid S onto the wall, then stepped back to inspect the effect. "Casey, what do you think?"

Casey joined Suzanne onstage and surveyed the row of bright paint jars in front of her. "It's pretty."

"Come on over when you decide on a color. There's room here beside me."

Casey looked around at the others. Abby had written her name in black, with red shadows all around it and a dark gray cloud encircling it. Neil was filling in his rounded, bright blue letters with cartoony faces, basketballs, and cars. Kate had made straight green letters that were very tall, with yellow rays emanating from them.

Megan was writing her name in multi-colored spirals with musical notes springing from each letter. Chris was filling in his dark blue block letters with bright M&M'S®, and Jeff had written his name in a beautiful Olde English script. The letters were muddy brown but in the center of each was an unmistakable streak of golden light.

Casey sighed. *How did they know what colors to use and what kinds of letters to make?* Slowly, still unsure of herself, she picked up a jar of purple paint and moved to the area of canvas between Suzanne and Jeff.

Suzanne was finishing the outline of her shiny yellow letters which were curved into one another, all connected. She began to fill in the first letter with alternating rainbow swirls of color. "That's beautiful!" said Casey, wishing she felt that way inside.

"Thanks. Yours will be just as beautiful." Suzanne nodded at the paint jar in Casey's hand. "Go ahead, get started."

"I don't think it'll be as nice as yours," Casey said doubtfully.

"That's not the point," said Marianne, coming up be-

61

hind them. Several silver bracelets jangled as she laid her right hand on Casey's shoulder. "It's not a contest to see who has the best-looking name. Just begin and see what happens. Have fun with it."

Casey tried to smile although she was still sure her graffiti name would look like a disaster when she was done. She dipped the brush tentatively into the dark purple paint and made the first strokes of a block letter C.

She stepped back to survey her work.

"Not bad," said Jeff, who had stepped back also. "Try making the outline come out a little wider. Like this." He dipped his brush in the purple paint and completed the C so it looked like a crescent moon.

"Hey, thanks! I like it!" Casey looked at Jeff gratefully, then pointed to his Olde English letters on the wall. "You're pretty good at this."

"Well, I'm an artist," he replied, moving back toward his name and adding some confident finishing touches.

Casey started working on the letter A. "Do you mostly paint?" she asked him.

"Painting and sculpting." He glanced over at her, wiping his hands on his jeans. "My art teacher says I'll get into Rhode Island School of Design, no problem."

"Wow, that's cool!"

"Right. Tell that to my dad." Jeff leaned back against the table. "He wants me to study business," he said bitterly as if "business" was a swear word. "Sometimes I freakin' hate him!" In frustration, he kicked the chair beside him, and Casey jumped, knocking over her jar of purple paint.

"Oh no! I'll help you clean that up," Jeff said, grabbing some rags from the table.

"Sorry," muttered Casey, her heart pounding in her chest as she still very still, watching him soak up the glistening purple puddles from the stage floor. "You scared me."

Jeff looked up at her and noticed her pale face. He shook his head. "I'm the one who's sorry," he replied. "My dad just makes me so angry sometimes."

Suzanne and a few of the others gathered around. "Everything okay?" Peter called from the piano, where he was going over the script with Marianne.

"It was an accident," Casey said, picking up a rag and wiping some of the paint off her legs. She went back to her name, her hands still shaking a little, while Jeff hurried to the kitchen to rinse out the rags.

Casey filled the large C with cooking utensils and the A with animals as best she could draw them. She had always thought if she could do anything in the world, she would be a veterinarian. Margaret, her best friend in West Hartford, had assorted cats, dogs, turtles, goldfish, and hamsters. One of the cats had had kittens when Casey was visiting, and she had watched them being born. That day, she'd almost believed in God.

Casey's father hadn't allowed her to have pets. She remembered with vivid clarity the day she had brought a stray white kitten home when she was seven. There had been an awful scene that night. He had blamed her mother for letting the kitten stay in the house until he got home from work. He was allergic, he had told her, why couldn't she remember that?

Casey had watched the whole thing, with seven-year-old terror, from the living room, including the part where her father had thrown everything he could get his hands on, and the part where her mother had tripped in her anxiety to get away from him, driving her arm through the glass kitchen door, tearing her arm wide open. It had taken 35 stitches to put it back together again, and she still bore the jagged scar, shiny and pink.

Her heart still pounding with fear at the memory, Casey suddenly realized that she also bore a scar from that evening, as deep if not as visible.

Mechanically painting lime green stripes into her capital S, Casey shuddered at the memory of the blood that evening. It had sprayed absolutely everywhere in the kitchen, even drenching the poor white kitten who had retreated, cowering, onto the windowsill. After they got back from the hospital, she and her father had scrubbed the floor and counters and woodwork for hours. In silence. Her father had unceremoniously picked up the kitten and dropped him outside the front door like a wad of trash. Casey had cried for days, worrying about what had happened to the poor little thing. And she had never asked for anything again.

"Hey, Casey! Wake up!" said Suzanne, snapping her

fingers in front of Casey's eyes.

Casey shook her head, scattering the ugly images of her past, happy for once to be back in the present moment.

"Peter's ready to start rehearsal," Jeff said, taking the paintbrush from her hand and laying it in a large can of water to soak. "You can finish this later."

Marianne began playing the lively "Prepare Ye the Way of the Lord" as Neil climbed onto the stage with a large empty orange plastic bucket and a bright yellow sponge. They began to sing the now-familiar tune.

"All right, everyone," called Peter from the floor. "Find some way to run around the stage without bumping into each other. Remember, you're like little children!"

The rehearsal proceeded around the piano for a few more of the group songs. Casey plunged right in with the others, singing with all her heart, letting the music lift her out of her current predicament and give her flight, like it used to.

She listened in wonder to some of the words. *When wilt Thou save the people? Oh God of mercy, when?* She did indeed wonder when God was going to save the people: Eric, her father, herself. She could really relate to the characters who were singing this song. They sounded like they'd had enough trials and troubles. But it also sounded like they at least believed in God, and a God of mercy, at that. She shrugged off her puzzlement and went with the tempo of the music. "Believe in the music," Peter had said.

That was all she needed to do right now.

The last song touched her with its simple, sweet melody. *All good gifts around us are sent from heaven above . . .* Casey sang these words with a hollow echo in her heart as she wondered. What good gifts? Her life seemed to be in such a ragged mess. She hadn't seen her father in months. Eric had just broken up with her. If she didn't finish this musical, she'd have a criminal offense on her record. She had no idea what was going to become of her life. And here she was, singing about *good gifts*?

All of a sudden, Casey looked up from the sheet of music. Her eyes found Suzanne, smiling as she sang, on the other side of the piano.

Was this one of the good gifts, she wondered? A new friend? She blushed then as she became aware of Jeff's warm gray eyes studying her as they sang. Another gift? She quickly lowered her eyes back to the music.

So thank the Lord, thank the Lord, for all His love . . . Casey felt a lightening of her heart, although she didn't know why. Perhaps everything was going to be all right after all.

"Y'all sound tremendous," Peter told them. "Take a ten-minute break, and then let's get back in a circle to talk about that homework assignment." Megan and Neil groaned. "I know, I know." Peter shrugged his shoulders in an exaggerated gesture. "No rest for the weary." They laughed.

Ten minutes later, as they were pulling their chairs into

a circle by the piano, they heard the outside back door of the hall open and slam shut, echoing loudly. The group turned almost in unison to see who had joined them.

Casey gasped. Eric was standing in the back of the hall.

CHAPTER 8

Casey's heart began to pound. Could Eric have changed his mind? Did he want to go out with her again? And what if he did? Would she go with him now? She chewed on the end of a broken nail and held her breath as Peter walked over and held out his right hand. "Hi, I'm Peter Wright," he said easily. "What can I do for you?"

Eric leaned against a table at the back of the church hall. He smiled slowly, ignoring Peter's outstretched hand. Then he looked straight across the hall at Casey. Peter let his hand fall to his side and followed Eric's gaze.

Eric called out. "Casey?" His voice was golden, familiar.

Casey shivered at the sight and sound of him, and not in the good way that she remembered.

"Casey. I need to see you for a minute." His words hung in the warm summer air. It was a command, not a request.

Casey sat up a little straighter and glanced at the others. No one saw anything wrong with this situation. Just a friend dropping by to say hello to a friend, she supposed they were all thinking.

She looked back at Eric. Did she really want to talk to him? She remembered how he'd held her, how safe she'd felt when she was with him, how good it had been at first. Maybe . . .

She stood and walked to Eric, smiling nervously at Peter. "It's okay," she told him. "This is a friend of mine. We'll just be a few minutes." Peter frowned and hesitated, then nodded and went back to the circle.

As soon as they were outside with the church door closed behind them, Eric pulled Casey to him and touched his lips to her hair. "Hi there," he murmured.

Casey nestled herself into his arms and felt her body relax. "Hi there yourself," she replied, lacing her fingers through his belt loops.

"I've missed you, babe," Eric whispered, framing her face with his hands and bringing his lips to hers. Casey melted into the kiss. In a minute, he let her go. "Want to go to the beach? I've got some good weed in my back pocket."

Casey stepped away from him. She looked down at the ground and then at the church before she met Eric's eyes again. "I can't, Eric. Really. No."

He smirked. "Come on, Case. You're not really having fun with these church kids, are you?"

Casey looked down at her feet and played with the hem of her lavender tank top. She thought of Suzanne's kindness, of how Jeff had confided in her, and how the others had simply accepted her. She remembered how, in the midst of all the singing and laughter of the rehearsal she had felt a new kind of happiness, a new belonging. And how she had felt safe, in a place that wasn't surrounded by Eric's arms.

"Look Eric, I really can't talk to you anymore. I'm going back in now." She reached for the door handle, but his strong, wiry hand stopped her.

"Wait. Casey." His voice was no longer smooth but edged with jagged desperation. Reluctantly, she turned to face him. "You have to help me," he said. "You have to come to court with me next week and be a witness."

"What?"

He squeezed her hand. "You've gotta tell the judge it was an accident. Last week. The party. You know. That I didn't mean to hit that kid so hard. It wasn't really a fight. You know that." He was slightly out of breath.

Casey stood very still, looking at Eric in confusion. She had never seen him so agitated, so worried. "I can't do that, Eric," she said quietly. "That's not the truth. I don't know why you were hitting him, but it wasn't an accident."

He stared at her, anger shining in his dark eyes. "Just do it for me, babe. I need you to do this for me."

"Eric, I told you—"

He rocked back on his heels and lit a cigarette, blowing smoke in her face. "That kid, he's in a coma. Doctors say he'll be brain damaged for sure. They don't know if he'll ever wake up. His parents are pressing charges." Eric was pleading now. "Please, Case. Help me out here, will ya?"

Casey sighed. She saw the others through the door's window. The blurred sound of their voices and laughter grounded her in reality. "I can't help you by telling lies, Eric. Not anymore."

She went back into the church and closed the door quietly behind her, but not without hearing Eric swear at her first, not without hearing his angry promise, "You're gonna be sorry, girl, very, very sorry."

When Casey took her seat again in the circle, the discussion stopped. "Everything okay?" Peter asked.

She sat on her hands and stared at the floor, pressing her lips together. What had she just done? She had never said no to Eric before. Not once. She'd had a chance to have him back again and she'd thrown it away. He had come to her for help and she'd shut the door on him. What was she thinking?

"Casey?" Marianne's light, silvery voice broke into her thoughts. "Peter just asked if you were all right."

Casey looked across the circle. She realized she was trembling and took a deep breath, letting it out in a rush. "I think so."

Megan leaned over and rested a brightly manicured hand on Casey's arm. "Want to talk about it?"

She attempted a smile, suddenly grateful for the love that seemed to be filling the circle, then shook her head.

"Okay then," Peter said. "Who wants to go next?" He handed Casey another copy of the drawing of the children. "Suzanne and Abby just told us they feel like the kid on the swing, like everything's going well for them and they're pretty happy with life right about now."

"I said I identified with the boy climbing the tree," Megan added, trailing her fingers through her dark hair. "Not because I feel like a boy . . ." They laughed. "But because I'm just starting to know what I'm good at and what I want to do with my life, and that feels good, and I want to keep climbing."

"That's as far as we've gotten," said Peter. "Who's next?"

Jeff ran his fingers through his thick brown hair, still studying the sketch in his hand. "That's me," he said quietly, clearing his throat and pointing to the boy standing at the top of the slide. "The one who looks so afraid. I wish it weren't me, but it's the only kid that I identify with. I know how that feels."

"How what feels?" asked Peter, leaning forward, elbows on knees.

Jeff cleared his throat again. "To be in a good place like that. Being in a good place and then not being able to . . ." He sighed. "I mean, just being afraid to take the next step and go any further."

"It's okay to be afraid, Jeff," Peter said gently.

"Right, right," he blurted out. "You've said that to me before. But I just . . . how can I take any steps forward when my father's standing in the way? It's this art school thing. I'm working so hard to be sure I get into RISD, and now he's telling me what a waste of time it would be."

"I think you're just going to have to be persistent," said

Peter. "Let him know you want to use the gifts God has given you."

Jeff nodded. "He's really mad that I did pre-applications this spring without telling him. He thinks I should go into business and high finance like he did. That's stupid, I told him. I always get D's in math. But I'm good in art." He paused. "Better than good."

"Maybe your dad thinks you don't value what he does," offered Kate softly, pushing her glasses up on her nose.

"Yeah," said Chris, popping a handful of M&M'S® into his mouth and offering the shiny brown bag to the others. "Maybe he needs to know that you think what *he* does is important, even though *you* don't want to do it too. My grandfather always says that God needs all kinds of talents for His world."

"Even businessmen and high financiers," added Marianne with a grin.

"Right. I never thought of that," said Jeff thoughtfully. "I'll try to talk to him differently next time. But whatever happens, I'm going to art school. Whether I'm afraid or not."

"I know a little bit about fear," said Marianne. "The thing to remember is that people who are courageous do things in spite of their fear. They don't wait for the fear to go away before they move forward. That's what courage is."

Neil stopped goofing off with Chris and studied Marianne for a moment. "*You're* afraid?"

She nodded, her long beaded earrings the only movement on her usually animated face. "Peter and I have been trying to have a baby for five years and it's just not happening. I'm really afraid that I'll never have children, and that's what I want more than anything. Whenever we go to a new doctor, I'm afraid that she'll tell us it's hopeless. Whenever a friend of ours has a baby, I'm so jealous and angry inside, I can't stand it. I'm afraid Peter will stop loving me if I can't have his children." She paused. "Yes, there's a lot of fear inside me. Some days are worse than others."

Casey was staring at Marianne in open disbelief. This woman who seemed so upbeat, so happy . . . *This* woman was afraid a lot of the time? She knew what *fear* felt like, the fear that twisted her stomach until she could hardly breathe? Casey hadn't thought that anyone else knew what that felt like.

"What . . . what do you do?" Casey asked, almost in spite of herself. "I mean when you get afraid like that. What do you do?"

"Well, I pray, first of all," Marianne replied. "I ask God to remove my fear. I ask Him to give me hope, and courage to go on."

"That's it?" Casey asked. "You just ask God to take it away?"

Marianne nodded. "And I also do something concrete, some kind of action that eases the fear. For instance, Peter and I have contacted a local agency about adopting a baby from South America. I still want our own baby, but going through the adoption process has helped me not to focus on the fear quite as much. As a matter of fact, in this picture of the children, I think I'm most like the ones on the seesaw. When I'm afraid, I'm like the child on the ground, but after I've asked God to remove the fear, then I'm the kid who's joyfully lifted into the air."

Casey was busy pondering all of this when Neil suddenly spoke up. "That's it!" He snapped his fingers and hit his forehead with the heel of this hand. "I've been blanking out when I looked at the drawing, but now it makes sense. Most of the time, I'm the kid on the seesaw, the one on the ground."

"The ground?" said Jeff in bewilderment. "You're always so full of energy, so positive, and always fooling around. I was thinking you'd be the kid in the air."

"Yeah, well . . ." he glanced over at Peter who nodded slightly. He took a deep breath. "I've never told you guys this before, but Peter knows. And Chris. My mom's an alcoholic and when I'm at home I have to take care of everything. Dad stays at work all day and half the night and I have to take care of just about everything—"

"But your mom comes with you to church every Sunday," said Megan.

"I know," Neil replied softly, staring at the floor for a moment, then meeting Megan's eyes. "It's hard for people to believe, but most of the week she's dead drunk, running around to the city bars, getting into trouble. The only thing she insists on is staying home on Saturday nights and walking into church sober on Sunday morning."

"But I thought you—" began Kate.

"Right. We look like the all-American family. Not." He shook his head sadly. "So usually I'm on the down side of that seesaw, even though I don't show it. I go to Al-A-Teen meetings a few times a week at the Methodist Church, and that helps a lot. A real lot. At least I know I'm not the only one dealing with this." He slumped back in his chair.

Chris interrupted the silence with his deep, comforting voice. "It must have been hard for you to tell everyone that." He raised the bag of candy. "Here's to keeping your seesaw up in the air."

Peter nodded in agreement and glanced at his watch. "Okay, guys. We've got about 20 minutes left. Let's finish up with the picture. Kate? Chris? Casey? Which child are you?" He raised his right eyebrow, waiting patiently.

"Well, I feel like that kid on the side, the one watching everything that's going on," offered Chris, lifting his left foot onto his right knee and playing with his shoelaces.

"Me too!" exclaimed Kate, looking at Chris with surprise. "I didn't know you felt like that."

"Well, you know, with my grandfather in the hospital and all—"

"He's in the hospital again?" asked Suzanne.

"Yeah. They took him back in this afternoon. The doctors say it's pneumonia this time. So all we can do is wait to see what happens next."

"You're pretty close to your grandfather, aren't you?" asked Peter.

Chris nodded. "I *was*. He's so sick now that he's never awake when I go to see him anymore." He swallowed hard and shook his head. "I'm like that kid on the playground. All I can do is stand in the background and watch."

"You could try talking to him anyway," suggested Kate. "I read somewhere that people who are in a coma or can't communicate because they're so sick can usually still hear what we're saying to them."

"Really?" asked Chris, looking at Peter.

"Absolutely," Peter replied. "I'll bet your grandfather would love for you to talk to him, even if he can't answer you."

"He'd probably feel less alone," offered Abby.

Chris rubbed his forehead. "Maybe I'll try that."

"Okay, Casey, you're next," said Peter, leaning forward in his seat.

Casey drummed her fingers on the side of her chair. "I think . . ." she began, looking up for a few seconds into the group, and back down at the floor. Then the words rushed out. "I think I'm the child at the bottom of the ladder."

"Tell us more," said Marianne.

"Well, I kind of want to climb the ladder," she replied, clutching the rounded edges of her metal folding chair. "But I'm afraid of what I'll see when I get to the top."

"Right, right. And you're probably afraid that when you get to the top, you won't be able to go any further," Jeff said with a grin.

Casey looked at him with relief. "Yes, that's it."

"That's exactly how I felt before I applied to art school. Too afraid to climb up, to try. But I did. And now I'm at the top of the ladder and I'm afraid to go down it. But I will, I know now that I can. And whatever you're afraid of, Casey, I know you can climb up the ladder too."

"Really?" She laughed nervously. "It looks awfully steep from here."

"Right. It is steep, but I'm sure you can climb it," Jeff said quickly. "Absolutely sure."

"I'm sure of it too," echoed Marianne. "Just ask God for help before you start. You don't have to do it alone."

Casey nodded. She couldn't speak, but her heart had stopped pounding.

"Okay, everyone. That leaves one more person!" said Marianne with a grin, poking Peter with her elbow. "Let's have it, dear. Which child are you?"

Peter groaned. "I thought I was going to get away with this one."

"No way!" said Neil indignantly, and the others laughed.

"Yeah, you made *us* do this assignment," said Megan with a false pout, pulling her long dark braid over her shoulder and pointing it at him. "It's only fair. Your turn now."

"Right," said Jeff, pointing to Peter's T-shirt. "Get serious."

Peter held up his hands as if fending off an angry mob. "Okay, okay. You win!" He paused, then frowned. "It was hard at first to do this—" he began.

"Sure," countered Neil with a grin. "Probably because none of those kids are wearing goofy T-shirts."

Peter chuckled. "Well, that too. But mainly because I identify with all of the children on the playground. I guess at one time or another I've been in all of those situations. When I was little, I was on the sidelines watching a lot. My real father died when I was just a baby, and then a few years later my mother remarried. We were very poor and my stepfather didn't want me around. I was on the sidelines a lot back then. My mother loved me and spent a lot of time with me, especially taking me to church and reading with me and all. But I wanted my stepdaddy to like me, at least spend some time with me. All he was worried about was the fact that we had hardly any money. I think he saw me as a financial burden."

"Geez, Peter," said Jeff. "That's rough."

Peter grimaced. "And that's not the half of it. One night when I was ten and my mom was visiting a neighbor, he came home from work in a really foul mood, and I'm sure he was drunk. He came at me with his black umbrella and thrashed my head and shoulders with it."

Casey gasped.

Peter looked over at her and nodded slightly. "It got worse. I tried to run out the door but every time I got near it, he got there first and blocked it. He made fun of me and called me a mama's boy and said all I was good for was church and school and coming between him and his wife. When Mama came in, I was in my room and he was still jabbing at me with the pointy end of the umbrella. I thought she was going to kill him. Lord knows, that's what I wanted to do. But she didn't. She looked him right in the eye and told him to leave. 'Leave and don't come back.' "

"Did he go?" whispered Casey.

"Yes, he went. And then my mother and I packed our things and went to her sister's house in Raleigh. I thought for the longest time that it had all been my fault, and I felt so sad and guilty listening to Mama cry at night. I know she loved him and that it had been hard for her to leave. My uncle told me one time that I couldn't have done anything different, that it wasn't my fault, that my stepfather was a sick man and needed help."

"Did you ever see him again?" Casey asked, her voice full of new boldness and insight.

Peter shook his head. "No," he replied softly. "But even now that I'm thirty-four years old, with a lovely, talented wife and a great church, even now I sometimes . . ." His voice shook. "Once in a while I wake up on Sunday with the dread fear that he is going to be sitting in one of those pews waiting to listen to me speak of forgiveness and love when I have never, ever felt either of those things for him."

The room was silent for a long, weighted moment. "But how *could* you forgive him?" Abby asked, her fists clenched in her lap. "How could you even begin to *love* him?"

"I don't know," Peter said, staring at the paper in his hands. "I'm an ordained priest and I can love all sorts of people I hardly even know, but I don't think I'm ever going to love my stepfather."

"I don't understand," said Casey carefully. "Why do you think you ought to love and forgive him after he hurt you so much?"

"Because Jesus told us to love our enemies," Peter replied. "And I believe in the power of what Jesus taught."

"Oh," said Casey, frowning, genuinely puzzled. "But how do you *love* your *enemies*?"

"Good question," said Peter. "I honestly have no idea. Yet. I think I'll pray about it and see what happens. Now, y'all really do need to get on home. Your parents are going to think we've kidnapped you!"

The kids stood and pushed their chairs back. They moved in closer together, arms around each other's shoulders, and said the Lord's Prayer.

And this time, Casey closed her eyes and whispered the words with the others, almost convinced that God would hear her.

CHAPTER 9

Later that night, on her way back from the bathroom, Casey stopped when she heard the sound of crying from her mother's bedroom. It was almost midnight; she was surprised that her mother was still awake.

She stood by the closed door, unsure of whether to knock and enter, or to pretend she hadn't heard. The last time she'd heard her mother crying had been the car ride that had taken them away from her father and to this new life in Woodfield. Before that, the only times she had heard her mother cry were when she had been bruised and beaten. Those cries were more desperate, painful even. The tears tonight were softer, interspersed with moments of trying to catch her breath.

Casey remembered those other times now, and with the memories came her own feelings of powerlessness and inadequacy. She had not been able to do anything for her mother all those other times. She had always stood, frozen with fear, unable to move. Perhaps this time she could make a different choice.

She tapped lightly on her mother's bedroom door.

Sunny's voice rose sharply out of the tears. "Who is it?"

"It's me."

"You should be asleep."

"I know. I'm just on my way to bed now. Can I come in?"

After a long moment, Casey heard the sound of sheets being pulled back and her mother blowing her nose. When Sunny opened the door, her anguished face softened. "Are you all right?" she asked, seeing the worry on Casey's face and drawing her close.

"I think I should be asking you that question," Casey said, holding on to her mother and feeling a sense of security she hadn't felt in several months, not even with Eric.

Sunny rubbed her red-rimmed eyes and tucked her beautiful auburn hair behind her ears. "You heard me crying."

"Yes."

"I'm sorry, Hon." She let go of Casey and motioned her into the room. Casey moved slowly across the worn patterned carpet and sat on the edge of the dark-rose canopy bed. This had been her mother's room when she was a teenager. Grandma Rachel had used it as a sewing room after Sunny had married Russell, but she had kept it pretty much the same. A heavy, shiny sewing machine still sat on what was once a handsome, sturdy desk.

Sunny sat next to her on the bed and blew her nose again. She sat silently then, shredding the tissue with worn, reddened fingers. Casey hesitantly put her arm around her mother, feeling her vulnerability. It both frightened and reassured her.

Sunny rested her head for a moment on Casey's shoulder and wept quietly again for a few minutes. Casey felt her own fear rise up inside of her and threaten to consume her. But this time she took a deep breath and silently asked God to take the fear away. What else was it Marianne had said? Let yourself feel it. Don't fight it. Do something positive. Act.

Casey stroked her mother's thick hair, dry from the summer heat. "I'm so sorry, Mom," she said softly into the nearly dark room. "About Eric. The party. The police station. Everything."

Sunny lifted her head from her daughter's shoulder. "I know," she said quietly, smoothing back Casey's hair. "It's okay. I've just . . . been so lonely lately. And now they've moved the court date up to August sixth and I don't know if I'm ready."

"August sixth? That's only three weeks away!"

"I know when it is," Sunny said with a sigh. "Will *you* be ready?"

"I don't know, Mom." Casey chewed her thumbnail. "I guess I'll have to be."

Sunny tossed the soggy tissues into the white wicker wastebasket beside the nightstand. "You don't have to do this," she reminded Casey. The sound of crickets blew in with the warm breeze through the open window.

"But I told you I would, and I will. I want to help you.

I love Dad but . . . I mean, I want to make up for all those times I *didn't* help you."

Startled, Sunny looked into Casey's eyes, reading there a bitter flash of regret.

"Oh, Casey, surely you didn't think you could have stopped him from hurting me all those times?"

Casey shook her head fiercely, slowly. "Maybe not. But I really, truly wanted to."

Sunny put her arms around her daughter. "That wasn't your job, sweetie. It was my job and I screwed up. I wish—" She quickly stopped. "I wish a lot of things. But don't ever blame *yourself* for not doing anything. It was up to *me* to do something. It's up to each of us to do something to protect ourselves. It was up to me to see that I was being hurt in the first place, to realize that I didn't deserve that, and to put a stop to it." She looked intently at Casey. "Don't testify in court for *me*, Casey. Do it for *yourself*."

Casey nodded, her eyes bleary now with repressed emotion and fatigue. She had no idea what her mother meant. She was to testify against her father, for herself? What did that mean?

She nodded again, too drained to continue this conversation, then stood, smoothing out her dark purple sleep shirt. "Okay, Mom. I'm going to bed now. Will you be okay?"

Sunny smiled wearily. "Sure. Good night, Casey. I love you."

"'Night, Mom. Love you too." She closed her mother's

door softly and walked quietly down the hall to her room. She studied the array of music boxes on her bureau, then picked up the *Wizard of Oz* scene that played "Somewhere Over the Rainbow." She wound it slowly, setting it back down on her nightstand beside the picture of her with her dad. She wearily slid under the sheet and rested her head on the pillow, watching the tiny porcelain figures of Dorothy and the others glide smoothly under and around the perfectly arched rainbow, over and over again.

The dream. It returned to her when she finally closed her eyes and slept.

She and Mom are on one side of the same riverbank. Her father is on the other side, screaming at them to come back, throwing rocks and heavy branches at them in desperation. This time Casey doesn't hide behind the nearest tree. She stands beside her mother and watches her father on the other side. Her stomach is churning concurrently with the river rapids, but she finds herself rooted to the ground, unable to move. She cannot go to him and she has no desire to hide.

Her father stumbles into the raging river, thrashing around, seeking something to hold onto, shouting for help. The waves churn and whirl around his bobbing head. He sputters, swallowing mouthfuls of water.

Casey feels someone beside her. She turns in her helplessness. It is a man, a tall bearded man, wearing a tie-dyed Superman shirt and worn blue jeans with red suspenders. He looks a little like Peter, but this man is older, darker, wiser.

"Help him! Please help him!" Casey cries, grabbing the familiar stranger's arm.

The tall stranger says nothing, but puts his arms around Casey and her mother, drawing them to him. The water calms. Her father is no longer there.

CHAPTER 10

"Blessed are the poor in spirit," Chris called from stage right. His "disciples" were seated in a semi-circle around the stage.

"Okay, Kate, that's you," called Peter from his director's chair on the floor in front of the stage. Kate jumped up. "Poor in spirit means you're empty, ready to be filled, waiting, so—"

Kate let her body go limp as a rag doll. She grinned sideways at Peter. "Like this?"

"That's good. Now Chris, tell her what the poor in spirit get!"

Chris moved toward Kate and gently straightened her up. "Theirs is the kingdom of heaven," he said jubilantly.

Kate beamed and clapped her hands like a little girl.

"That was great! Now, everyone—do you remember which 'blessed' you are?" They nodded. "Okay, then, go for it!"

Chris moved once again into the gentle character of Jesus. "Blessed are those who mourn . . ."

Abby jumped up and took her hands away from her eyes.

". . . for they shall be comforted."

Abby acted surprised, then threw her arms around Jesus with joy and relief.

"Blessed are those who hunger and thirst for righteousness."

Jeff dragged himself across the floor, panting and clutching his throat, his eyes wide with fear.

Chris crouched down and felt his forehead. ". . . for they shall be satisfied."

Jeff looked up at Jesus in confusion for a moment, then jumped up, grinning and rubbing his stomach like he'd just eaten a five-course dinner.

"Blessed are the peacemakers . . ."

Neil stood up and tried to shake hands with Kate on one side of him, then Megan on the other. They ignored him, arms folded defiantly across their chests.

Chris/Jesus ran behind Kate, then Megan, bopping them both on their heads and shaking his finger at them in turn, then making a sign of the cross on Neil's forehead. ". . . for they shall be called the sons of God."

Acting ecstatic, Neil offered his hand to Kate and Megan again. This time, they were smiling too, and shook his hand with exaggerated strength. Peter chuckled.

"Blessed are the merciful . . ." Casey stood up and wiped her sweaty palms on her dark blue jogging shorts. Merciful. Had Peter given her this particular "blessed" on purpose? She went down on one knee, bowed her head and folded her hands, willing herself not to think about her father.

Chris/Jesus walked in front of her, cupped her chin in his palm and raised her head slowly until her eyes met his. He smiled at her. ". . . for they shall obtain mercy." Casey was stunned for a moment, frozen yet melting inwardly, looking up at Jesus's kind eyes as mirrored through Chris.

Chris cleared his throat. "For they shall obtain mercy," he repeated with deliberate slowness.

Casey blinked. *Oops, almost missed a cue!* She quickly rose and held tightly to Chris/Jesus's hands, smiling broadly.

"Rejoice and be glad, for your reward in heaven is great."

Peter clapped. "Hey, I really liked that scene. You guys are gooooood!"

Chris bowed as he mock-saluted Peter. "Thanks, boss. What's next?"

Peter waved his notebook in the air. "Scripts, everyone, scripts!" They grabbed their notebooks and sat on the edge of the stage. When they had settled down, Peter said, "We won't be rehearsing any songs tonight. Marianne's not coming."

"Everything okay?" Abby asked with concern.

"Actually, she has an appointment with our contact from the adoption agency. We've been waiting for several months now, and finally got a call yesterday. They think they have a baby to place with us."

Everyone gasped and cheered at once. "Peter, that's awesome!" said Jeff.

He nodded happily. "She's over there now, seeing the pictures, getting the details. So we have the rest of rehearsal tonight to work on some scenes. Let's start with Abraham and Lazarus. Okay?"

After several more scenes, they took a break. Casey sat on the edge of the stage, swinging her heels against the wall. The others had gone to the convenience store down the street for something to drink. "Bring me back a root beer," she told them, insisting she wanted to stay inside to be alone for a few minutes with her thoughts.

Staring off into the brightness of the large church hall, she tried to imagine it the night of the show, filled with folding chairs, filled with people. Where would her mother and Grandma Rachel be sitting? Would they like the show? What if she forgot her lines? Would her father be there? She chewed on an already short pinky nail and clenched the edge of the stage tighter with her other hand. Wait. Did she even *want* him to be there?

"Yo, Casey, wake up!" Suzanne's voice broke through Casey's cloud of apprehension.

Casey blinked. "You're back early." She accepted the chilled can of soda, holding it against her cheek and savoring its icy shock for a moment before popping the lid and taking a long, bubbly swallow.

"Everyone else is in slow motion back there at the store. I figured if I stuck with them, your soda would be warm by the time we got back here. So, I put it into high gear for you."

Casey grinned. "Well, thanks."

Suzanne reached behind her and wrapped her thick, brown hair into a ponytail, then twisted it into a barrette on top of her head. "Besides," she said, sipping her bottle of water. "You told me before rehearsal that you wanted to ask me something."

"Oh, right." Casey fiddled with her watchband. "My mom and I are going to see *Cats* next week in New Haven. Do you want to come?"

Suzanne jolted the plastic bottle down on the stage and the water splashed up and out of it. "*Cats*? Are you serious?"

Casey nodded, grinning at Suzanne's obvious pleasure, attempting to wipe up some of the water with a tissue from her purse.

"Of course I'd like to go. I've been wanting to see it forever. Thanks!" She sipped her water again. "Any special occasion?"

"My birthday."

"Next week?"

"No, not until the middle of August, but *Cats* is here next week, so we just decided to—"

"You'll be sixteen then?"

Casey nodded. "When's your birthday?"

"December eighteenth. I can't wait! I'll be able to get a job then. Mom and Dad said when I was sixteen, I could get a job. You know—a real job, not like babysitting or anything. So I can start saving money for Divinity School."

Casey picked up her script and fanned herself with the loose pages. "You're lucky, knowing what you want to do with your life already."

"I've known since I was twelve. How about you?"

"When I was little, I wanted to be a veterinarian. I love animals. I used to go to my friend Margaret's house all the time because she had pets all over the place. I think I loved them more than she did."

"Didn't you have any pets?"

Casey drank some soda and went back to fanning herself with the script. She stared at the can, suddenly ashamed. "My father wouldn't let me." She glanced up quickly at Suzanne who was watching her intently, patiently. "I was thinking about that yesterday," she said, her voice still lower. "At rehearsal, when you had to get my attention to stop painting my name on the wall."

"Thinking about what?"

"About the first time I brought home a stray kitten and asked if I could keep it."

"What happened?"

"He . . . my father . . . Well, he was allergic to cats, and I didn't know that, but he . . . he blamed my mother for letting me bring it into the house." The rest of the story tumbled out of her mouth faster than she could catch it. "He was so angry that he said all kinds of horrible things to my mom, and he threw things at her and she tried to get away and tripped and her arm smashed right through the kitchen door and we had to take her to the hospital and she had thirty-five stitches and she still has the scar." Her eyes filled with tears, but she willed them back, and listened to the hammering of her heart in the heavy silence of the church hall. She couldn't believe she had just told Suzanne all of that.

Suzanne set her drink carefully down on the stage and leaned closer to Casey, putting one arm gently around her. "It's okay. Really, it's okay."

Casey shoved her away and stood, knocking over the drinks and scattering the scripts in the process. "But it's not okay. Don't you see? It never was okay! He hurt my mother, not just that time, but lots of times."

Suzanne quickly stood up and went over to her new friend, putting her hand on her shoulder. Casey covered her face with her hands. What would Suzanne think of her now? She hadn't meant to tell her all of this. She hadn't meant to shove her away. She could hear the others outside on the sidewalk in front of the church: Abby's high-pitched giggles and Jeff's full-throated laughter. "I'm sorry," she whispered, wiping her tears away with her hands, and then onto her shorts. "I shouldn't have told you any of this."

Without a word, Suzanne pulled Casey's stiff, unyielding body closer and held her for a moment. "It's okay that you told me, Casey," she said firmly, gently. "It's an important part of your story. We all have a story . . . and I still like you."

Casey felt Suzanne's warmth all around her, even after she had let her go and they were picking up the scattered script pages from the stage. Funny, it had felt the same in the dream when the stranger had put his arms around her and her mother. It had felt the same when she looked up into the eyes of Chris's Jesus a little while ago, in the middle of that scene from *Godspell*.

"Hey, you two, what's going on in here?" called Neil as the others burst into the hall. He tried to imitate Peter's deep voice and southern accent. "Let's get this stage cleaned up, ladies!"

The others laughed as they helped Suzanne mop up the spilled drinks and put the scripts back together. Casey was still shaken by what she had just revealed. She was amazed that Suzanne hadn't backed away from her in horror when she had told her about her father.

"Okay now," said Peter, who was the last to join them on stage. "Let's try the Miracle Worker scene."

They took their places. Kate stood up on the old sawhorse, now painted fluorescent orange, and began talking to the audience, straining to make her voice louder. "Christ performed many miracles. One day, He came into a small town and found a person struck with leprosy."

Abby dragged herself across the stage, with a pitiful look, reaching into the air. "Help me! Please! Cure me!"

The others raised their fingers, pointing to the sky as they chanted, "Look! It's a bird! It's a plane! It's Super Christ!"

Chris/Jesus leaped out from behind the ladder, landing with a thud in the midst of the teenaged disciples. "That's me!" he shouted. He pointed down at Abby, who clutched his leg in desperation. "You, Ms. Leper, are cured!"

Abby immediately jumped up, studied her arms and legs for a moment, showing elated surprise, then bowed deeply and raced back to her place in the group.

"That same day, Jesus came upon a girl who could not see," continued Kate from her perch above the others.

Casey stumbled out to center stage, her eyes closed, hands in front of her, feeling her way. "I can't see! I can't see!" she moaned loudly. It was hard to keep from smiling at the irony of her being placed in this scene. She knew the feeling: not being able to see, not understanding. It didn't necessarily have anything to do with physical blindness at all.

"Louder," called Peter from his chair on the floor.

"Sorry . . . I can't see! I can't see!" Casey shouted again as loud as she could. She ran smack into Chris/Jesus, almost knocking him over.

"What's the matter with you? Are you blind?" Chris/Jesus asked somewhat sarcastically as he grasped her wrists.

Casey nodded her head vigorously, as Peter had suggested in the previous rehearsal.

"Then open your eyes!" Chris/Jesus commanded.

She opened her eyes as wide as she could get them to go. The others shouted "POOF!" and the scene fairly oozed with melodrama. Casey turned her head, this way and that, trying to give the impression that she could see again. Then she cried, "My hero!" and hugged him quickly before running back to her place in the group beside Megan and Jeff.

She was panting and smiling when she flopped down. She felt light and almost weightless, as though something heavy had been lifted from her shoulders.

"Hey, that was sweet!" Jeff whispered, leaning over while Suzanne began dragging herself across the floor in her role as the lame person. "You're the perfect blind person!"

Casey laughed out loud, then clapped a hand across her mouth to stifle the noise. "Thanks Jeff," she whispered back. "You don't know how right you are!"

After rehearsal, as they were getting their things together, Jeff stopped them. "Hey guys, wait up! Does anyone want to go to the carnival after rehearsal tomorrow night?"

"Oh! Fun!" said Abby.

"Yeah, sure!" Neil grinned. "I can give any clown there a run for his money."

"Or *her* money!" said Abby. They all laughed.

"We're going to visit my grandfather again tomorrow night," said Chris, looking toward the door. "But maybe I could join you later."

"Count me in," said Suzanne. "How about you, Casey?"

"I'll have to check with my mom. I'm not sure if I'm still grounded or not."

Neil gave a low whistle. "Grounded, huh? What did you do, rob a bank?"

"None of your business, wise guy," Suzanne said.

"No, wait," Casey interrupted. She was surprised at her courage, which seemed to well up inside of her from a deep, sweet spring that she had been unaware of until right this moment. "I don't mind telling you." She took a deep breath. "I was at this party with my boyfriend, Eric, and we got busted because he got into a really bad fight. There were drugs and alcohol at the party, and when my mom came to pick me up at the police station, she was pretty upset. Besides which, I wasn't supposed to even be out with him. So basically, that's why I'm grounded."

The others were silent.

Casey looked around at these faces which had become so familiar. She tentatively explored the silence, and finding only acceptance, she reached into it and came up with more courage. "It wasn't the first time it happened. Which is also why I'm doing *Godspell* with you guys this summer."

Jeff frowned. "Right. But I don't get it. What does *Godspell* have to do with that party you were at?"

Casey took another deep breath. "My mother and grandmother go to this Church. And Mom was so upset she didn't know what do to, so she brought Peter with her and he made a deal with the cops that if I did some time in his Youth Group this summer, nothing would go on my record. I didn't have much choice. At first, I was really mad that I had to spend so much time here with you guys. But now . . ." She smiled. "Now I'm really glad about it. This is more fun than I thought it'd be."

"But what about Eric?" Abby asked.

Casey ran her fingers lightly along the keyboard for a moment. "He's . . . well, that was him who came to see me last week at rehearsal. I'm not supposed to be seeing him anymore. And I don't really want to."

"What did he want?" asked Jeff, studying Casey with a new intensity.

Casey hesitated, then took a deep breath. "He wanted me to go to court for him and tell the judge that the way he hurt the boy at that party was an accident and not intentional."

"How bad was he hurt?" Kate's voice was on the edge of a whisper.

"Eric beat him up pretty bad," Casey said, staring at the piano keys, then holding on to the bright yellow piano for support. "He's in a coma."

"That's terrible," said Jeff. "But what did you tell Eric about going to the judge and all?"

"I told him no," she replied softly.

The others broke into applause. "Good for you, Casey! Way to go!" She stared at them for a moment in disbelief, then the reality of their support broke through to her and she laughed right along with them. Good for her, indeed.

"Do you think your mom will let you go with us to the carnival tomorrow night?" Suzanne asked Casey as they started to walk home a few minutes later.

"I'm not sure. Maybe. She might. She thinks you guys are good for me." Casey grinned. "And she's right, of course."

Suzanne smiled too as they walked the rest of the way in comfortable silence.

On the sidewalk in front of Casey's house, she stopped Suzanne before she walked away. "I really want to thank you for listening to me during the break tonight. I never told anyone that stuff before, about my father and all."

Suzanne shook her head. "It's okay, really, Casey. It helps to talk about things like that."

"You'll be a great minister someday," Casey replied seriously. "I mean it."

"Well, thanks." They sat down on the porch steps, shoulder to shoulder.

"Can I tell you something else?"

Suzanne nodded.

"My mom is going to court on August sixth for the divorce, and she wants me to tell the judge how my Dad used to hit her."

"Oh Casey, that's—"

"Well, really, she told me I didn't have to do it, but how could I not? He hurt her so many times, and I could never help her then, but this . . . this is a way I can help her now. Except . . ."

"What?"

"Except she told me last night to testify against my father for myself, and not for her. I don't understand it. What do you think that means? How can I do it for me and not for her?"

Suzanne tilted her head back and frowned at the wide

black sky, glistening with stars. "I'm not sure, Casey. May-be just that if you do go and tell the truth, you'll be less likely to let the same thing happen to you."

"What?" Casey felt ripples of anger burning into her chest and clutching at her stomach. "How could you even think that? I would never—" Suddenly a scene flashed be-fore her eyes. Eric. At another party. Someone had teased him about his new haircut, and he'd gone absolutely ber-serk. Like a tornado, out of control, he'd destroyed what-ever was in his path: books, shelves of CDs, plants, beer bottles . . . and his best friend Lonzo, who'd had a black eye for a week.

Casey clapped her hand over her mouth and looked at Suzanne in dismay. "I just realized—"

"What?"

"It's just . . . Eric. He . . ." She stared at the ground and bit her thumbnail.

"Did he ever hit you?"

"No," Casey said quickly. "Not me. But others. I saw him . . ." She shook her head. "He never hurt me." She paused. "At least, I don't think so. But then, that's what I used to think about my dad."

"There are lots of ways to hurt people," Suzanne re-plied. "Hitting is just one of them."

Casey studied Suzanne's kind face for a moment. "You're right," she said thoughtfully. "My mother told me that once, but I didn't understand it then."

They were quiet for a few moments, looking out across

the grass, listening to the noisy crickets in the still summer night.

"I'll go with you if you want," Suzanne said, breaking the silence and standing as she stretched. "On August sixth. When you go to court."

"You will?" Surprise filled Casey's voice.

"Of course. If it were me, I'd want a friend there."

Casey stood too and moved toward the front door. "Thanks. I'd like that."

"Okay. Good night, Casey."

Casey bounded into the house with a new energy, eager to talk about the rehearsal, eager to ask her mother about the carnival. Eager to start over.

CHAPTER 11

"No, no! Get that away from me!" Casey doubled over with laughter, pushing Neil away from her. He waved a frothy pink cone of cotton candy in front of her nose. "I've had enough. I just might throw up if I eat anything else!"

They had been at the carnival for almost an hour now, and Casey couldn't remember when she'd had more fun. Just then, Jeff and Abby came up behind her, and Jeff covered Casey's eyes with his hands. "Guess who?" he said, winking at Neil and Suzanne over Casey's head.

Casey felt warm, strong hands against the side of her head. "Jeff?" she said breathlessly, still holding her side from laughing so hard with Neil.

"How'd you know?" complained Jeff, letting his hands linger on her shoulders for a moment.

"Must've been your pizza breath!" laughed Neil.

"Hey!" Jeff punched him playfully in the arm. "Take that back."

"Will not."

"You'd better!"

"Make me!" Neil turned and ran off, Jeff close at his heels.

"Boys!" said Abby in mock disgust. "Sometimes they act like three-year-olds."

"And sometimes we love it, don't we?" said Suzanne, grinning at Casey, who was still gazing after Jeff.

Abby nudged Casey. "I think he likes you."

"What?" Casey quickly refocused on Abby and Suzanne.

Suzanne nodded in agreement. "He likes you. Jeff."

"No." Casey stared at them in amazement. "Really?"

"Do I detect a note of hope in her voice?" Suzanne looked at Abby, her voice full of teasing.

"I think so," replied Abby.

"Oh, come on," said Casey. "How do you know he likes me?"

"We have our ways," said Abby mysteriously. "I'm two years older than you, remember? I know all about stuff like this!"

Casey looked from one to the other. It seemed too good to be true. The carnival, the friends, and now this. Jeff liked her too. She shook her head. "I don't know . . ."

"You'll see," said Suzanne. "Hey, want to go on The Snake?"

Casey looked behind her at the towering roller coaster on the other side of the parking lot, glittering with red and white lights, twirling people upside down and backwards in open air cars. "No thanks. My stomach couldn't take it," she said. "You guys go ahead. I'll just wander."

"You're sure?" asked Abby. "I love The Snake. It's my favorite carnival ride."

"No, really. I'll ride the Ferris Wheel or play a few games or something. Go on. We'll meet later."

"Okay. 10:00. Right here?"

"Sure. What about Jeff and Neil?"

"Oh, they'll catch up with us, don't worry." Abby and Suzanne headed toward the roller coaster.

Casey walked around for a while, absorbing the carnival sights and sounds. Occasionally, she stopped to try her hand at one of the games, seemingly guaranteed to deplete her quarters. She got lucky at one booth where she had to toss her coins into moving multi-colored sailboats. "A leopard for the little lady," said the toothless old man who ran the booth, presenting her with a large stuffed leopard, all honey-golden with chocolate brown spots and a rainbow striped tie around its neck.

She looked into the leopard's eyes as she walked away. Triumph surged in her heart. "You and I are going to be friends," she told him, then held him close to her body, feeling the furry warmth even through the night's humidity.

Suddenly, someone's hands covered her eyes, startling Casey so that she dropped the stuffed animal, waving her arms blindly in front of her. "Jeff? Is that you? Jeff?"

The hands dropped roughly to her shoulders and twisted her around. Suddenly it wasn't just fear clutching at her throat. It was Eric's hands. He shook her, hard. She could smell beer on his breath.

"Jeff?" he said, mimicking her hopeful voice. "Jeff? Just who the hell is *Jeff*?" His rage bellowed in the thick night air, his face so close to hers she could see the shiny drops of saliva in between his teeth. "Answer me! Who the hell is *Jeff*?

"Let . . . me . . . go!" Casey managed to gasp. Eric flung her out of his grasp, and she stumbled backwards, grazing her elbow in the dirt. She tried to get up, but he bent over her and slapped her across the face.

"I said you'd be sorry, girl. Now you're gonna be sorry."

Casey lifted herself up on one forearm and looked wildly about her. They were at the back edge of the fairgrounds, between a deserted hotdog stand and the woods. Why wasn't anyone else here?

She began to scramble up, looking for an escape. But he shoved her back in the dirt and tore at her green tank top.

She tried to push his hand away and they struggled until she collapsed under his violent strength. "There we go, nice Casey," murmured Eric, his voice quieter now, his hands less rough as they found their way to the zipper of her white shorts. "See, this is gonna be fun now. Nice, sweet Casey."

She tried to scream but found she had no voice. Then she remembered her mother. All those times her mother was so helpless. What was it she had told her the other night? *It's up to each of us to protect ourselves.*

Casey turned her head away from Eric's agitated gaze. Out of the corner of her eye she saw the stuffed golden leopard, lying abandoned in the dry grass. Further back, she imagined seeing a tiny white kitten- helpless, dependent, streaked with blood. "No!" she screamed suddenly, lifting both of her feet and kicking Eric in the stomach with all her might. He thudded backwards into the dirt. Quickly, with strength she didn't know she had, she scrambled to her feet and ran to the toy leopard, gasping for breath. She grabbed it in her arms and zipped up her shorts, then limped quickly away, leaving Eric still on the ground, clutching his stomach and groaning in pain.

After several minutes of wandering the fairgrounds in a daze, oblivious to people's stares, continually looking over her shoulder, Casey ran into Jeff and Neil whose usual jesting vanished at the sight of her beautiful red hair tangled with dried old leaves, the dirty white shorts, the bleeding knee and elbow. "Casey, what happened?"

Still clutching the leopard, she let Neil put his arms around her. Jeff stood by helplessly as she sobbed, letting the fear pour out of her. They were still standing this way when Abby and Suzanne found them.

"Casey! What's wrong?" cried Suzanne, rushing up to them in dismay. Casey didn't move. "Casey? Casey!" She gently put her hands on her shoulders and turned her away from Neil, who seemed greatly relieved that female reinforcements had shown up. "Look at me, Casey. Tell me what happened."

"Eric," Casey whispered. "Eric found me."

Jeff clenched and unclenched his fists. "Where'd he go? Tell me where he went," he demanded, his voice rising.

"I'll knock him down so hard he won't know what hit him."

Casey looked at him, startled by his devoted fury. "That's okay," she replied, suddenly feeling like herself again, centered and anchored in the midst of these new friends. "I already did that."

"Say what??!!" Abby exclaimed, chewing her gum furiously. "You knocked him down?"

"Yes," said Casey, loosening her grip on the leopard. "I knocked him down." The thought of Eric, wind knocked out of him, on the ground by the hot dog stand brought a flicker of amusement to her eyes. She giggled. "Pretty amazing, huh? I knocked down Eric, big bruiser Eric." Then she burst into laughter.

Bewildered, they laughed with her. "But Casey, are you all right? Do you need to see a doctor?"

"No, I don't think so. He knocked me down and slapped me a few times," she replied carefully. "Then I tried to scream and I couldn't. But I thought of my mother and how she . . ." She saw Neil, Jeff, and Abby looking at her in confusion. "How she used to let my dad beat her up." She looked away. "And I couldn't let Eric do that to me too. So I found some strength I didn't know I had, and I kicked him in the stomach." She stroked the leopard's head. "Hard," she added.

Jeff grinned. "Well, good for you!" he said, his words soft and sure. "I'm proud of you."

Casey looked at him as she straightened the leopard's colorful bow tie. "You know what? I'm proud of me too."

CHAPTER 12

Sunny and Grandma Rachel were sitting on the front porch that night when Abby dropped Casey off. Rachel's voice stopped in the middle of a sentence as soon as Casey stepped into the dim light of the porch.

"Casey?" Sunny stood up quickly at the sight of her disheveled daughter, and her voice was full of sharp distress. "What on earth happened to you?"

"Mom, I'm okay," Casey began, brushing some more dirt off of her shorts and settling into the porch swing beside Sunny. "Really. I ran into Eric at the carnival and—"

"Eric?" Sunny's voice raised several decibels above normal. "I told you I don't want you hanging around with him anymore." She looked down at Casey and shook her head angrily. "I trusted you out late tonight because you were supposed to be with the kids from Grace Church." Her voice held many layers of disappointment.

"Wait a minute! I *was* with the kids from Youth Group. Eric found *me*! I wasn't hanging around with him." She glared at her mother. "Why don't you just trust me for once?" She gripped the golden leopard tightly to her and stood, shaking her mussed hair back from her face. "I'm going to take a shower and then go to bed. Good night." She kissed Grandma Rachel quickly on one soft cheek and ran into the house and up the stairs, slamming her bedroom door as loud as she could.

She leaned against the door for a moment, her legs and stomach suddenly trembling at the memory of what had happened at the fairgrounds. Eric loomed in her mind, the sting of his hand slapping her face, the terrifying powerlessness of being knocked to the dirt. She held the stuffed leopard tighter and kissed its soft, furry head as tears came to her eyes. Eric had hit her and abused her. He'd been ready to hurt her even more. What would she have done if she hadn't met the kids at Grace Church? What would she have done if she hadn't found the strength and courage to protect herself against him? For she knew now that he would have hit her sooner or later, even if she had said yes to him outside of the church that night a few weeks ago. Would she have had enough belief in herself to fight back? Would she ever have dared to fight back? She thought not.

Casey slumped to the floor and sobbed into the leopard's fur.

After a while the tears subsided, yet Casey remained on the floor, holding the leopard loosely in her arms, staring dimly into her room. She hadn't made her bed that morning and the purple and white batik bedspread was crumpled on the floor. Slowly, she eased herself up and crawled over to the bed, intending to pull the covers back on.

Something caught her eye instead. Protruding from under the bed was her black leather guitar case. Instinctively, she reached for it and slid it out. It made a silky sound against the smooth green carpet.

She set the leopard on the floor beside her. "Look at this," she said to him. She carefully snapped open the case and ran her hand tenderly over the glossy wood. "This is my guitar." She hadn't touched it since that last night in West Hartford.

She stroked it for a few minutes, then gently eased it out of its case and rocked it in her arms as though it was a poor motherless child. The warmth of it against her body brought back memories of happier times with her father.

She moved it into playing position and the familiarity of holding it this way rushed back to her with joy. She let her fingers toy with the strings and was jolted back into reality by the harshness of the flat sound.

"Guess I'll just have to tune you up a little, won't I?" she murmured as she began adjusting the strings.

Soon it was reasonably tuned, and Casey began strumming a few chords. She suddenly grinned with pleasure as the "Edelweiss" song came back to her, and she sang it softly, remembering the night when she was eight and her parents had taken her to see *The Sound of Music.*

She continued to strum the chords, humming the tune softly under her breath, enjoying the sense of peace that was washing over her.

In the midst of this, she heard a gentle knock at the door. "Come in," she called, still strumming the guitar.

Sunny cautiously opened the door and peeked in, smiling briefly when she saw her daughter sitting cross-legged on the floor, playing the guitar. "I thought I heard music up here."

Casey nodded, her eyes on her fingers as they strummed.

Sunny walked into the room and sat on the floor beside her daughter. She picked up the leopard and patted him. "Who's this?"

"Just something I won at the fair."

"He's beautiful. Did you name him yet?"

Casey shook her head, then set the guitar back in the case and eased herself up off the floor, wincing at her stiff, tender muscles.

"Casey, I'm sorry," Sunny said quickly. "I should have trusted you."

"That's okay, Mom," Casey replied, sitting on the edge of the bed and covering her mouth as she yawned. "You heard me say 'Eric' and you went crazy. It's understandable. All things considered."

"Forgiven?"

"Forgiven." Casey rubbed her elbow.

Sunny perched on the edge of the bed next to Casey, studying her daughter carefully. "What exactly happened?"

"He . . . he knocked me down and hit me a few times. Just trying to make me sorry that I said no to him the other day."

"You saw him the other day?"

"Yeah, he found me at rehearsal and asked me to go to court with him to tell the judge that his hitting that kid at the Fourth of July party was an accident." She looked at her mother. "I said I wouldn't do it, and he got really mad."

Sunny shook her head in disbelief. "But tonight . . . How did you . . . How did you get him to stop hitting you?" She inspected Casey's bruised knee.

Casey smiled, remembering. "I kicked him in the stomach," she replied. "I kicked him so hard that he couldn't get up, and then I ran and found the others."

Sunny stared at her in bewilderment. "You *kicked* him?"

"Yeah, Mom, I kicked him. I remembered what you told me the other night about how it's our job to protect ourselves, to realize that we don't deserve to be abused, and then do something to stop it." She paused. "So I did. I stopped it. I don't know. I just suddenly realized how strong I was . . . and then my feet did the rest."

Sunny bit her lower lip and clasped her hands together. There were tears in her eyes. "You really stopped him," she said slowly, and this time it was a proud statement rather than a question.

Casey nodded.

"Well, I hope he learned a lesson," Sunny finally said, smiling broadly.

"Me too" said Casey. "Don't mess with *me*!" They laughed. "And I guess someday I'm going to have to forgive him." She paused. "Just not right now."

"Well," Sunny said. "This has been quite a summer so far, hasn't it?"

Casey grinned, pulling the bedspread back onto the bed. She took the leopard from her mother. "Friend," she murmured into its soft fur before setting it down on the pillows. "I'm going to call you Friend."

Sunny headed for the door. Then she turned and faced Casey. "I'm glad you're playing the guitar again." She leaned against the old maple bureau and glanced down at the array of music boxes. "It's been a long time since we've had music in our lives."

"I know." Casey bent down and eased the guitar back into the case.

"Are you going to play for *Godspell*?"

"I think so," Casey said, shutting her guitar case with a snap and standing it beside the bed against the wall. "I'll just need to practice a lot. Megan wants me to do 'Day by Day' with her, and they told me I can do 'By My Side' if I want to." She wound up the "Over the Rainbow" music box on her nightstand and watched it for a moment, savoring the thin notes sparkling quickly through the room. "I didn't think I could," she said. "But after tonight, I think I can do anything!"

Sunny leaned over and kissed Casey gently on the top of her head. "I think you're right," she agreed.

"Mom?" Casey asked, as her mother got to the door.

"Yes?"

"How did you stand it? I mean . . . Dad . . . hitting

you all those times. How did you stand it?" She shuddered, rubbing her sore shoulder.

Sunny shook her head, sadly traced the long scar on her forearm, then looked at Casey. "I don't know," she said, her voice almost a whisper. "I really don't know. I loved your father. So much. I kept thinking and hoping he would change."

"But he didn't."

"No, he didn't."

"And Eric's not going to change either. I'm glad you got me involved over at Grace Church. It's made a difference."

"I've prayed that it would," Sunny replied, a new peace settling over her. She kissed Casey's forehead. "Good night, Hon."

Casey hummed "All Good Gifts" to herself as she got ready for bed.

❦

CHAPTER 13

"Hey, look!" Megan said with excitement when Casey and Suzanne walked into rehearsal the next night. "Casey brought her guitar!"

"What?" said Peter, standing up from where he'd been crouched on the stage, painting purple polka dots on the sawhorse. He shielded his eyes as though from the sun. "Well, I'll be . . . It is! Look everyone! It's a bird . . . It's a plane . . . It's Super Casey and her guitar!" He jumped off the stage with a thud. His bright yellow Big Bird T-shirt was spattered with purple splotches of paint.

Casey laughed. She was still limping a little from her run-in with Eric, but she felt stronger and more centered than she ever had before. Lifting the guitar in a gesture of triumph, she said, "Yes, it's me. I thought I'd see if I could learn some of the music. If it's still okay, that is."

The others applauded. Marianne came up to Casey as she set the guitar against the yellow piano. "It's more than okay, Casey," she said softly. "We're glad you're going to play for us."

"So, how'd it go the other night at the adoption agency?" Neil asked. "Are you two parents yet?"

"Well . . ." said Marianne, looking hesitantly at Peter.

"As a matter of fact, we are!" Peter said, grinning happily. "Her name is Angelica and she's two weeks old. Marianne is going to fly to South America next week to meet her and bring her home."

"All right!" Neil cried. They all reveled in the celebration for a moment.

"I'm going to take a leave of absence from the Symphony," Marianne told them. "But I'll continue to play for you guys until *Godspell* is over."

"Hear! Hear!" said Abby with delight.

"Oh, I don't think you'll be hearing me with the baby, I think you'll be hearing the baby!" They all laughed.

"Okay, okay," Peter finally said. "Let's get back to rehearsal." He looked at the group gathered around the piano. "Anyone seen Chris? Or Jeff?"

The others shook their heads. "I think Chris went to visit his grandfather again," Neil said. "He was pretty sick yesterday when I went with him."

"Oh, no!" murmured Kate and Megan almost at the same time.

"Well, let's say a quick prayer and get started," suggested Peter. They quieted down and bowed their heads. "Jesus, please be with Chris and his family tonight as they are present beside his grandfather Joseph. Grant them peace in the face of their sadness, and Your holy, healing presence in the face of pain and death. In your name, we ask it. Amen."

The others murmured their Amens.

"All right. Since Casey has brought her guitar today, let's start with "Day by Day." Megan? Casey?"

They moved to the stage and the others formed a semicircle behind them. As Peter was explaining the scene, giving stage directions to the others, Casey tuned her guitar carefully. Absorbed in the process, she didn't see Jeff come in and crouch down behind her.

"Are you all right?" he whispered.

Her head jerked up, then she turned and saw him. "Oh, hi!" she said, her eyes shining. "You're always startling me."

Jeff brought out a small bouquet of hand-picked violets and buttercups from behind his back. "Then I guess I'll have to keep with tradition." He handed her the flowers and took his place with the others in the background.

She stopped tuning her guitar, buried her nose in the purple and yellow flowers, then turned again to smile at him. She mouthed the words "thank you," then turned back to the guitar.

"I'll fill in for Chris," Peter was saying. "Megan, you can come over here and kneel by me. We'll leave Casey sitting over there on the wooden crate to play the guitar while she sings."

Megan moved to where Peter sat on the edge of the stage.

"I think candles would be nice here, don't you?" Marianne asked from the piano bench.

"Candles?" asked Suzanne. "Could we each hold one?"

"Good idea," said Peter, looking at the kids assembled before him. "This is a solemn song that you're singing to Jesus. It's a point in the show where you've all just begun to understand who He really is. Candles would be very effective."

"Hey!" said Megan excitedly, combing her fingers through her hair. "What if, at the beginning, Jesus has the only lit candle. And then, as it goes on, we could all light our candles from His."

"Megan, that's perfect!" said Peter. "Now, let's go. Casey, are you ready?"

She nodded. "I have to use the music, though."

"No problem," said Peter. "Just as long as you're not using it the night of the performance!"

Casey shook her head. "Don't worry. I'm a fast learner."

She began to play then, strumming the simple chords and then listening to Megan's clear soprano voice rise above the music:

Day by day, day by day
Oh dear Lord, three things I pray:

Megan raised her forefinger and slowly glided it in to meet Peter/Jesus's forefinger.

To see thee more clearly,

She pulled her hand back, then raised her forefinger and index finger, gliding them in to meet Peter's.

Love thee more dearly,

Three fingers meeting three fingers now.

Follow thee more nearly,

Day by day.

Casey riveted her eyes back to the music and played louder while Megan danced slowly with Peter/Jesus. Then they settled back down on the floor and looked over at Casey, who softly, softly began to sing the words over again.

Day by day, day by day...

"Louder, Casey, we can't hear you," called Peter across the stage. She heard him as if in a dream. She breathed in deeply, raised her voice, and continued.

Oh dear Lord, three things I pray:

Peter gave her the thumbs-up sign. She could hear her voice harmonizing with Megan's, and she sang the rest of the song with her eyes closed, enjoying the words, singing it like a prayer.

To see thee more clearly,

Love thee more dearly,

Follow thee more nearly,

Day by day.

The others applauded and Casey opened her eyes, grinning at her success. "I did it!" she said, in awe. "I did it!"

"And you did it very well, too!" called Marianne from the piano. "Keep it up, Casey!"

Later, Jeff came up to her as she was waiting for Suzanne to finish talking with Peter. She held the flowers in one hand, the guitar case in the other. She smiled when she saw him and brought the flowers to her face, inhaling deeply of their earthiness. "These are beautiful, Jeff," she said. "Thank you again."

"I'm glad." He ran his fingers through his short dark hair. "Casey, would you . . . I mean . . ." He blushed. "Do you want to go to a movie with me on Saturday night?"

Casey blushed too, fingering the small petals of the violets. "I'd like that," she said softly. Jeff smiled and shoved his hands in his pockets as he happily walked away.

"Hey, what time?" she called after him.

He turned and smacked himself on the forehead, blushing bright red. "Right, right. How about 6:30?"

"Okay, great."

He was several feet away this time before she remembered something else.

"Jeff?"

He turned again.

"Do you know where I live?"

He grinned sheepishly. "Uh . . . no. But I'll call you later and get directions."

"Okay. Bye."

She giggled a little as she walked over to Suzanne and Abby, who were waiting for her by the door.

"And what have we here?" teased Abby. "Flowers?"

"Did we tell you, or did we tell you?" asked Suzanne, as they walked out to Abby's car.

"You told me, you told me," said Casey. "I just thought it was too good to be true!"

They laughed for a moment, then paused as Abby searched for her keys. "So, are you all right and everything?" Abby asked, dumping the contents of her denim purse on the hood of her old green car. "I mean after . . . the carnival?"

Casey nodded. "I'm just sore. But I'm healing already."

"You have a great voice," said Suzanne as they finally got in the car. She twisted around to see Casey in the back seat. "And I'm so glad you decided to play the guitar. It makes the show so much more . . ."

"Musical?" Abby asked, laughing.

"Yes, that's it, just the word I was looking for!" They all laughed.

"Have you guys memorized all your lines yet?" Casey asked, perched on the edge of the back seat, the flowers still clutched in her hands.

"Some," said Suzanne. "How about you, Abby? You've been in more plays than we have."

"I know some of my lines," said Abby. She glanced over her shoulder at Casey. "Don't worry. It'll all come together by opening night."

"We hope and pray," sighed Suzanne. "I'm just really worried about Chris. It's not like him to not call if he's going to miss a rehearsal."

"I bet he's at the hospital with his grandfather," said Casey. She glanced at her watch. It was 9:30.

"Hey!" said Suzanne. "Let's go see him." She waited for a response, then looked over at Abby whose face seemed paler in the darkness. "Abby?"

She shook her head quickly. "I don't think they'd even let us in, okay? It's way past visiting hours."

"But we could try," Casey said. "Please, let's try. He might want to see some friends right now. If his grandfather really is dying."

Abby shook her head again. "The last time I was in a hospital? It was the night that Preston died." She tightened her voice. "I don't think I can do it again, okay?"

"Did any friends of yours come to see you that night?" Suzanne asked gently

"No," Abby replied, leaning her head against the window, her voice far away. "I was alone. Even my mom and dad didn't get there until hours later." She repeated wearily, "I was alone." They rode in silence for a few minutes through the deserted streets, then stopped at a stop light. Abby looked over at Suzanne, then back at Casey. "Chris shouldn't have to be alone, should he?"

"His family will be there," said Suzanne. Her voice was soothing. "So we don't have to go if you really don't want to. We understand."

"No," Abby said suddenly, with a vivid new strength. "You're right. He shouldn't be alone. Let's go." The light turned green and she stepped on the gas, a determined look on her face.

Abby led them tensely into the fluorescent-lit hospital emergency room, blinking at the sudden glare of lights.

They walked up to the sterile white counter where a

weary-looking gray-haired nurse sat, typing on a computer keyboard. Abby put her hand over her mouth and looked away. The memories were flooding back too quickly. Suzanne put an arm around her and gestured for her not to worry. She cleared her throat. The nurse looked up and smiled faintly, taking an indulgent sip from a chipped coffee mug.

"How can I help you?" she asked, her voice surprisingly full of energy and life.

"I know you can't let us in to the hospital now, but a friend of ours is here because his grandfather's dying and we were hoping that you would page him for us." Suzanne stopped speaking to catch her breath.

The nurse looked at the three girls with interest. "Sure, I can do that. What's his name?"

"Chris Forrester. Could he meet us here?"

"Cafeteria would be better, Hon," the nurse replied, scribbling the name on a sticky note and reaching for the phone. "Too much stuff going on here sometimes." She smiled apologetically.

"No problem," said Suzanne. "Just tell us where it is."

"Okay," interrupted Casey. "You get directions. I'm going to call my mom and tell her where we are." She pulled her phone out of her pocket. Abby and Suzanne waited for her on a blue plastic sofa. A *Law and Order* rerun played to an absentee audience from a television suspended in the corner of the waiting room.

"You okay?" Suzanne asked, lifting a section of the

frizzy blond curtain of hair that hung around Abby's face.

She nodded and sighed. "I just keep thinking about Preston, you know? I mean, we weren't in *this* hospital or anything, but it reminds me of . . . Oh Suzanne, I was so terrified. . . ."

"I guess this is what Marianne meant when she said to ask God for courage even when you're afraid," said Suzanne as Casey joined them and they headed down the hallway to the cafeteria.

Abby looked at Suzanne in amazement. "You know, I forgot about that." She grinned and shook her head. They reached the cafeteria in time to hear a crisp, male voice come over the intercom. "Will Chris Forrester please report to the cafeteria? Chris Forrester please report to the cafeteria."

Casey giggled as they bought sodas and sat down at a glass-topped table near the window. "He's not going to have any idea who is paging him or why. Do you think he'll come?"

They didn't have long to wonder. Abby was the first to see him, standing in the doorway, looking perplexed and pale. He scratched his pimply forehead and yawned. He looked around the seemingly deserted cafeteria again and began to turn away.

"Chris! Wait!" Abby cried, jumping up and running to him, followed by the others.

"What the—" He swallowed hard and looked at them in amazement. "What are you doing here?"

"We kidnapped Abby while she was driving us home from rehearsal," Suzanne explained lightly, taking Chris's arm and steering him to their table. "Sit down. Can we get you something to drink?" He shook his head. "Eat?"

He patted his flat stomach and looked over at the food counter. "Maybe a sandwich," he replied. "I'll take it back upstairs with me."

They went to the counter and he ordered a turkey sandwich.

"How's your grandfather?" Casey asked.

He shook his head. "He's dying. The doctor said he probably won't make it through the night. My mom and I are staying here until he—" He took the sandwich from the cafeteria worker and turned away, wiping his eyes.

Abby took Chris's free hand. Some of her color had returned. "We just didn't want you to be alone," she said softly. "Neil said he thought you were here, so we decided to come and see if you were okay. Do you need anything else?"

He shook his head.

"Do you want Peter to come?" Suzanne asked.

"He was here already. Left a few minutes ago. I think I'd better go back upstairs now." He headed for the door, then turned to them. "You could come upstairs with me," he said hopefully.

The girls looked at one another doubtfully. "Do you really want us to?" Casey asked.

"It'd mean a lot to me, and to my mom," he said.

"We've been doing what Kate said to do the other day. Remember? About people in a coma still being able to understand what we're saying? So we've been telling Grandpa stories." His face took on some color and light. "Hey, I know! We could sing some of the *Godspell* songs for him. I've been telling him about it. He wasn't so sick when we started rehearsals, and he thought he was going to be able to see the show, but now . . ." His voice trailed off and he stared at the sandwich. "You don't have to," he began. "I know it's late and all . . ."

"We'll do it," said Abby, compassion for Chris emboldening her. "Casey even brought her guitar to rehearsal tonight and we have it in the car. Let's get it."

Chris smiled gratefully. "Thanks, guys," he said softly. He followed them to the car, and then they walked together to his grandfather's room in the special hospice unit.

Abby's face paled at the sight of the aged, frail man lying in the metal hospital bed, a pale blue sheet pulled up to his neck. His arms lay bony and fragile at his sides. Several tubes and needles protruded from his veins, as well as his nose and throat. His breathing was raspy, even with the aid of the oxygen. The heart monitor over the bed showed fluorescent green lines of sharp mountains and valleys, erratically alternating with long, level plateaus against a black background.

Casey and Suzanne studied Abby, then smiled down at Chris's mom who was silently pulling a needle of pale-yellow thread in and out of a cross stitch design. Tears gleamed in her heavy-lidded eyes at the sight of the girls, and she brushed a tired mop of limp curls off her forehead. "How sweet of you to come," she said. "Papa, look who's here." She spoke to the old man on the bed as if he were awake. "Chris's friends from Grace Church. They're doing *Godspell* together." She noticed Casey's guitar. "And they're going to sing for us, Papa, isn't that nice?"

Chris leaned in over his grandfather on the other side of the bed. "Grandpa, this is Casey and Suzanne and Abby. They came to keep me company for a while. We're going to sing some of the songs from *Godspell* for you, okay?" He laid his hand on his grandfather's loosely wrinkled arm and stroked it for a moment.

So they sang. They sang and rehearsed the different scenes amidst laughter and solemnity until Mrs. Forrester noticed the heart monitor had suddenly gone extremely erratic. She quickly ran to the door and called, "Lynne! Nurse Connors! Come quickly!"

A tall nurse with short brown hair appeared immediately in the doorway. Casey, Abby, and Suzanne moved to the back of the room and watched silently as Lynne adeptly adjusted the wires and tubes, then felt Joseph's forehead. "It's time," she said to Mrs. Forrester. "He's almost gone. Say your goodbyes now and then I'll come back." She hugged her for a moment. "It'll be okay, dear."

Chris and his mother moved in closer to the bed. "Papa, I love you," she said, kissing him on his deeply lined cheek. "Goodbye. Go with God."

"Grandpa, I love you," Chris said, tears streaming down his cheeks. "I love you." He clasped both of his grandfather's feeble hands in his. His mother quickly moved to Chris's side of the bed and put her arm around her son.

Casey wiped the tears from her own eyes and looked at Suzanne and Abby. "Should we leave?" she whispered. Suzanne shook her head no. Abby tightened her grasp on the chair she was leaning against.

Just then, Chris's grandfather opened his eyes. They were watery but they were blue, like Chris's, and they were filled with light. Chris and his mother gasped. "Papa?" she said, her voice quavering.

"Grandpa?"

Joseph smiled then, but not at them. It was the delighted smile of a toddler who has suddenly seen the most delightful surprise in the distance. "I have to . . . go home . . . now," he said through little gasps of oxygen. "Home. Going home." He smiled again, then closed his eyes for the last time.

Mrs. Forrester held her hand over her mouth for several long moments as she and Chris stood watching him. The room was filled with a strange and lovely silence.

An hour later, the girls were on their way home. It had begun raining while they were in the hospital, and the windshield wipers made rhythmic little swishing sounds against the drizzle.

"I'm glad we went," Abby said finally. "It wasn't easy, but I'm glad we went."

129

"Me too," agreed Casey, yawning and stretching out on the back seat.

"I've never seen anyone die before," Suzanne said carefully, toying with the silver ring on her right hand. "I've never even known anyone who's died before."

"Grandpa Bob died," said Casey. "Grandma Rachel's husband. But I was only five or six, and my father wouldn't let us go to the funeral."

"He didn't let your mother go to her own father's funeral?" asked Abby in disbelief.

Casey shook her head. "I don't remember much about it all, except Mom has always said she should have gone anyway."

"What an idiot," said Abby. "Your father. How could you live like that?"

"I don't know." Casey looked out into the night. "We just did. It's not like I had a choice or anything. I was just a little kid."

"But you're away from him now, right?" Abby glanced back at Casey.

"Right. And in two weeks I'm going to testify against him at their divorce hearing."

"That'll be hard," said Abby, turning off the highway at the Woodfield exit.

"I thought it would be, you know? At first, I didn't really even want to. I was just doing it for my mother. But lately, I've been thinking that . . . I don't know . . . I used to miss him and wish he would say he was sorry so we could start over and stuff. But now I'm kind of glad Mom has the restraining order. I don't know what I'll do if he convinces the judge that it's okay to see me again."

"But he *is* your father," said Suzanne, trying to understand. "You did say that you had good times, too."

Casey sighed as the car came to a stop in front of her house. "Yes," she said slowly. "But every good time in the world doesn't make up for how he hurt my mother. And me," she added, getting out of the car.

Carrying her guitar and the now wilted flowers into the house, she was surprised at her words and of how certain she was of their truth

CHAPTER 14

At the funeral for Chris's grandfather, Casey sat comfortably between Jeff and Suzanne in one of the rear pews of the church. It was crowded, and they could see Chris and his family up in the front, near the altar. Chris's blond head bobbed over the four smaller blond heads beside him in the pew.

Casey had been inside Grace Church only once before, on Easter morning when her mother insisted she attend the family service. On that occasion, the church had been dressed in a gloriously festive array of what seemed like acres of tall white fragrant lilies.

Now Casey noticed, except for the two singular lily plants on either side of the altar, the church was simply a church. Sunlight streamed through the colored glass windows, throwing stains of muted purple, blue and green onto the burgundy carpet. The pews were made of a smooth, light wood, lined with deep-blue cushions. A plain silver cross hung suspended in the middle of the space above the altar.

Neil, Kate, Megan, and Abby squeezed into the pew in front of Casey, where an elderly couple and a young woman were talking quietly among themselves.

Six men dressed in light summer suits commanded their attention as they slowly carried the large dark coffin down the aisle. The organ continued in the background, its usually strident sound muted and distant.

When the men had placed the coffin in front of the altar and returned to their pews, the music stopped, and the church was bathed in silence. The organist ruffled through the pages of her hymnal, then rested her hands on the keyboard and began the opening hymn.

Standing, Casey reached for a hymnal and turned to the correct page. She stared in bewilderment. "It's an Easter hymn," she whispered to Suzanne. She looked up at the hymn board near the lectern and rapidly flipped through the hymnal, finding the other hymns. "They're all Easter hymns."

Suzanne nodded, pointing briefly to Peter, who was now processing down the aisle with the acolytes and chalice bearers. "He's wearing his white stole and robe, too, like he does on Easter," she whispered in reply.

"But why? This is a funeral. It's not Easter."

"Listen to the words. You'll see," Suzanne said, smiling as through she had a secret.

Still puzzled, Casey frowned and began to sing with the others.

The strife is o'er, the battle done,

the victory of life is won;
the song of triumph has begun.
Alleluia!

Casey glanced at Suzanne, continuing to sing the rest of the Alleluias in the chorus. Easter songs at a funeral. A ripple of understanding coursed through her. Chris's grandfather had died, but he was alive in Christ, so he had only died to this earthly life. She briefly flashed back to the *Godspell* scene where Jesus dies on the makeshift wooden boards that they nailed to form a cross. The "disciples" weep and moan and dance in despair and grief as they carry him away.

Casey sang out the alleluias with more fervor on the last verse, remembering the final *Godspell* scene where Jesus joyously jumps out of the tomb and they all sing "Long Live God" with rollicking rhythm instead of the solemn sadness with which they had buried him.

Casey smiled and nodded at Suzanne as they put their hymnals away and listened to Peter begin the service. She hoped that Chris understood this, too. She hoped that his loss was woven with the same joy and hope that framed the Resurrection.

The next few weeks at rehearsals, Chris was quieter than usual. He played his role of Jesus with a tenderness that enabled him to contain his sorrow.

"No, Chris," said Peter impatiently. "This is the scene where Jesus overturns the moneychangers' tables in the temple. You have to act angrier than that." He rubbed his chin and tried to think of a way to inspire Chris to display more anger. "Let's start over. Listen, Chris. It's like these people are having a gigantic yard sale in the middle of our church, and none of them care that it was really built to worship God. Wouldn't you be angry?"

Chris nodded wearily, and they began the scene again. Casey took her place with the fluorescent green hula hoop and twirled it over her head as they all began shouting their carnival hawkers' wares. "Get your peanuts here!" "Five games for a quarter!" "Step right up, ladies and gentlemen!" They were loud and raucous, caught up in the revelry and competition of the scene.

Slowly Chris plodded across the stage, looking at each of them curiously, listening carefully as they shouted their wares, their games. When he reached the opposite end of the stage, his voice suddenly thundered at them with the now familiar line. "It is written that my house should be a house of prayer and you have made it a robber's den!" This time his vocal cords strained with the impact of the words and sweat formed in glistening droplets on his forehead.

They froze in place as he shouted this at them, and then he began to sing *Alas for You*. They stared at him, then quickly tiptoed around the stage, putting the toys and carnival props away, whispering to one another with the beginnings of pretend fear, and continually looking over their shoulders at him.

Casey didn't like this scene. Every time she heard the fringes of anger in Chris's voice, she was reminded of her father. Still, she knew that Jesus did get angry. It was right there in the Bible. The Pharisees and tax collectors hadn't understood what the temple was for. They had no idea who Jesus really was. He had felt their ignorance, their vast indifference, and He had been angry about it.

Blind guides, blind fools,
the blood you've spilt on you will fall.
This nation, this generation
will bear the guilt of it all....

Chris's voice picked up speed and volume as he remembered with abrupt force the empty place at their dinner table, the now quiet room at the end of the hall. And there were so many of his friends who didn't understand because they'd never lost anyone close to them.

Alas, alas, alas...
Blind fools!

His voice spilled over with rage as he screamed this last line of the song at them, his face reddened and contorted with anger.

Casey shivered and bowed her head. They all looked away from Chris/Jesus, acting like they were too ashamed to meet his accusing gaze.

"Bravo!" called Peter from the floor. "Chris, you're getting the hang of it now."

Somewhat dazed, Chris looked down at Peter. He could still feel his rapid heartbeat from the exertion of his anger. He nodded. Neil came over and patted him on the back. "That was good," he whispered. "Give us hell. We like it that way!" Chris laughed wearily and punched Neil in the arm.

"Shoot, we deserve it!" said Megan, coming up behind them and easing herself off the stage and onto the floor, her dark hair lifting behind her in the air for a moment, then cascading down her back.

They gathered around Peter and Marianne at the yellow piano. "Only three more weeks until the big day," said Peter. "We need to talk about a few things before then. Props for instance. Costumes. Publicity."

"I have my costume already," said Neil.

"Me too," added Kate and Suzanne.

Chris tugged at the sleeve of Peter's royal blue T-shirt. It had a huge yellow and red "S" on it. "About that Superman shirt you're wearing . . ." he said, chuckling.

Peter began to pull the shirt out of his plaid shorts and over his head.

"Not now, Peter," said Neil, pinching his nose in mock dismay.

"Yes Chris, you can borrow it," Peter said, chuckling as he tucked it back in. "And I'll be sure to wash it first! Now, the rest of you need to get some odd assortment of clothes together and bring them in on Tuesday. We want to be sure everyone has what they need."

"Remember," Marianne said, tucking her right leg under her on the piano bench. "It's supposed to look thrown-together, like you're all children who have been outside playing and you've just come together. Like a party."

"A come-as-you-are party," Casey added, surprised that she remembered. She liked the idea. *Come as you are.* She looked around at their faces. She had done exactly that. She had come to them as she was, and they had accepted her instead of trying to change her. Yet she had changed anyway.

"Also, next Tuesday, we're going to be making posters for the neighborhood," Peter was saying. "So, it's important that you all be here."

Casey realized with a start that next Tuesday she would be in court, testifying against her father. Fear gripped her stomach for a moment as she tried to imagine standing before the judge and saying those dreaded words out loud. *My father used to hit my mother. Many, many times.*

She swallowed hard. "I . . . I'm not going to be here on Tuesday," she said. "I'm sorry." The others were curious as they looked at her. "That's the day of my parents' divorce hearing. I have to go and testify . . . against my father."

Suzanne nodded, remembering her promise. "And I told her I'd go with her, so I can't be here on Tuesday either."

Peter looked from one to the other and nodded slowly. "Then you two are definitely excused on Tuesday. No problem."

"The rest of us will get the poster-making started without you," said Marianne. "Unless of course I have to go to South America to pick up Angelica. In which case—"

"In which case we'll create magnificent posters without you," said Jeff, grinning.

Later that afternoon, Casey pulled all the clothes out of her dresser drawers and surveyed the mass of T-shirts, tank tops, jeans and shorts before her. A costume. How was she going to put together a come-as-you-are costume?

Grandma Rachel poked her white-capped head around the door frame. "What on earth?" she exclaimed, coming in and eyeing the clothes all over the floor.

"I'm trying to create a costume for *Godspell*. It's supposed to look childlike and thrown together. Like I was caught off guard or something. Nothing's supposed to match." She picked up a tie-dyed green shirt and draped it against her neck, frowning. "Suzanne is wearing her dad's old pajama bottoms and her brother's letter sweater and a floppy felt hat she found at a yard sale last week. It looks really cool." She put her hands on her hips and stared at the mess helplessly.

Rachel clapped her hands together in childlike delight. "I have an idea. Can I help?"

"Can you *help*?" repeated Casey. "I need some *major* help." She frowned at the mounds of clothes.

Rachel grabbed Casey's hand. "Follow me," she said mysteriously, pulling her down the hall and up the stairs to the attic.

Once there, she sat Casey down in a dusty, oversized arm chair that was covered with a faded flowered sheet, then switched on the overhead light. Casey blinked and wiped her forehead. It was stuffy and hot. "I've never been up here before," she said, looking around her at the stacks of boxes, ornate picture frames, and covered furniture.

"First time for everything," Grandma Rachel said cheerily, kneeling on the creaky floorboards next to a tattered wooden trunk, now caked with dust. "I've got some things here just right for my 'Only's' costume!"

Casey giggled as she watched her grandmother open the trunk. Grandma hadn't called her that in a long time.

Peering into the musty-smelling trunk, Rachel reached in and pulled out a handful of material, piling the soft fabric onto her lap. "A shawl," she said, flinging its elegantly patterned oriental design around her soft, full neck. "A pair of pantaloons." She tossed the pale green gossamer-like pants over to Casey, who tugged them on over her jogging shorts, delighting in their silken softness and their billowy sweep against her long legs in spite of the heat.

"Perfect. What else?" Casey's eyes were shining.

"Rag skirt. White blouse." Rachel continued, holding up each item for their mutual admiration. "Felt slippers. Another shawl."

"Were these yours?" Casey asked, reaching for the bright green cotton scarf which was peeping over the edge of the trunk.

"Some were mine, some belonged to my mother," she responded, bringing out with a final flourish a long, colorful sheet with dancing animals all over it. "This was your mother's when she was little." She handed it to Casey.

"Oh look!" she exclaimed, pointing to the monkeys, the lions, the bears. "There are leopards dancing! Can we make this into a blouse maybe? And I can wear the green scarf around my shoulders. And . . . Oh!" She stood up excitedly, holding the sheet to her chest, then flinging the scarf around her shoulders. "I can carry 'Friend' with me onstage. And then all I need now is . . ." Her lively hazel eyes darted around the attic. "Something for my hair . . ."

"How about violets and buttercups?" teased her grandmother, sitting on the floor, legs splayed out, studying her 'Only' with amusement. "That would be the perfect finishing touch!"

Casey giggled and dropped to the floor next to Rachel, hugging her impulsively.

They hurriedly put the rest of the clothes back in the trunk and headed for the stairs, chanting, "Violets and buttercups, violets and buttercups."

"By the way," Rachel said later, helping Casey put away the piles of clothes on her bedroom floor. "Jeff called while you were out this morning."

Casey paused. "Jeff?"

"Yes, Jeff," said her grandmother, whisking the T-shirts out of Casey's hand and setting them back in the last empty drawer. "Remember Jeff? Of the violets and buttercups?"

Casey grinned. "What did he want?"

"I think he wants to be there at the divorce hearing with you tomorrow," she replied, fanning herself with the *Godspell* script which was lying on the bed.

Casey slowly picked up the Brahms Lullaby music box on the dresser and wound it up tightly, listening to the delicate notes running quickly together. Soon, the notes came less hurriedly, until the melody was playing at the proper speed. She hummed the simple tune for a moment.

"Do you think it's okay? If he comes, I mean." Casey looked at Grandma Rachel expectantly.

Rachel gently picked up the animal-printed sheet and headed for the door. "Do you want him there, my Only?"

Casey smiled and nodded, listening to the music box's melody fade away into stillness. "I like him a lot," she said, a mixture of hope and fear in her voice, her heart.

"Then let him be there for you."

"Suzanne already said she would be there. I invited her for breakfast."

"Ah, but we never can have too many friends around us, can we?" Rachel asked wisely. Casey looked at her in surprise. "I'm going to start sewing this blouse for you now, dear. Let me know if you need anything else, okay?"

Just a large dose of courage, Casey thought, grabbing her phone from the bed so she could return Jeff's call.

CHAPTER 15

Casey was so nervous on Tuesday morning that she got up while the first light of morning was lifting the night sky. She quickly pulled on her jogging shorts and an old Yankees T-shirt and left the house for a walk.

She hadn't slept much, but she was wide awake. This was the day she would face her father and he would have to listen to her tell the judge the truth. She picked up the morning paper from the sidewalk, intending to set it inside the front door for her grandmother, when the headline caught her eye.

ATTACKED YOUTH DIES — ERIC D'ANGELO ARRESTED FOR MURDER.

Casey felt her stomach plunge as though weighted with cement. She stood, rooted on the porch in the dim morning light, and read the article from start to finish. He had died. The boy at the party now had a name. And an obituary. Kevin Sanderson of New Haven. Age 17. Dead of head injuries received during a fight at a party on July fourth. Casey shuddered, remembering the blood, the ambulance attendants, Eric's blank stare.

"Eric D'Angelo, 19, of East Haven, administered the blows to Sanderson's head which caused a coma, then death. He was arrested late last night and taken into custody by the State until his hearing this morning in New Haven City Hall."

There was a photograph of Eric, her once beloved Eric, being handcuffed outside his parents' house. He was staring at the photographer with a mixture of scorn and angry defiance.

Trembling, she set the paper down inside the front door and set out on her walk.

Passing the still-darkened houses of her neighborhood, she crossed over Main Street and continued past the quiet shops and markets. Walking quickly now, a faint breeze easing the damp humidity of the morning, she headed for the cove at the end of the street.

Silently, she sat on one of the great granite rocks, overlooking the small harbor. The waves lapped peacefully around the smaller rocks below her. The tide was coming in. She held her long coppery hair off her neck and let the salty breeze lick her damp skin.

Fear lapped around her as well, edging its way into her mind, her heart. Not only was she going to have to face her father today, she might run into Eric as well. Their hearings were on the same day, in the same place. A tremor of fear shook her body as she remembered Eric throwing her to the ground at the carnival. Did she have anything to say to him now? Was there anything left to say?

She shook her head and stood, jumping off the massive boulder onto the soft sand, threading her way among the small stones and shells on the beach. Silently, she stooped and picked up a small green piece of sea glass. Its irregular shape reminded Casey of a lopsided heart. She brushed off the sand and rubbed her fingers over its smooth surface. Love, she thought when she studied its clear beauty. Love.

Casey gazed into the soft golden light filtering through the clouds. She prayed silently. *God. Please take this fear away from me. And if you can't take it away from me, help me to do what is right anyway. Help me to get through this hearing today.* She held up the green sea glass, as though showing it to the sky, to her God. "*I need you, God. I need you.*" She whispered these words aloud, still crouched in the sand.

Home again, the morning sun shining full strength now, she was greeted in the kitchen by Suzanne and Jeff. "You're up early," said Jeff as Casey came in, wiping her feet on the back porch mat, and brushing the sand off her shorts.

Casey smiled at the sight of them around the kitchen table. Suzanne, pouring maple syrup on her butter-laden pancakes; Jeff, cutting a banana into perfect round circles and dropping them onto his now-empty plate; Grandma

Rachel, at the stove, a gingham apron tied around her waist; her mom, opening the refrigerator and taking out another carton of milk.

"I went for a walk," Casey said, taking her plate to the stove and letting Rachel heap several pancakes onto it.

"Did you see the paper?" Jeff asked, gulping his orange juice. Casey nodded. "I'm glad they locked him up," he said fiercely. She nodded again, not meeting his eyes, slowly spreading butter on her pancakes.

Suzanne ate a forkful of pancake with obvious enjoyment. "Rachel, this is really good. Can I have the recipe sometime? My mom can't cook at all. She even ruins leftovers."

Casey's grandmother laughed and untied the apron. "Anytime, Hon. Eat up now. It may be a long time 'til lunch."

"So Casey, are you ready?" Suzanne asked later, as they sat on the front porch waiting for Sunny to pull the car out of the garage.

Casey looked at Suzanne and Jeff. She smiled. The small, hard, core of fear was still there, in the pit of her stomach. But it hardly seemed real. It was slowly being replaced by a singular core of strength that had been born that night at the carnival with Eric.

"Yes, I am," Casey said with new confidence. "I'm ready."

The divorce hearing did not take as long as they expected. Casey told her story briefly in a strong, steady voice that held no trace of fear. Was this courage, she wondered, as she met her father's indignant eyes across the spacious courtroom? Was this courage—being afraid and doing the right thing anyway?

She breathed a sigh of relief when her part was over. As she sat down, Jeff and Suzanne squeezed her hands and whispered that she did a good job. Her mother turned around from her seat in front of them and smiled, tears in her eyes. This was not easy for her, either.

Fifteen minutes later, Casey and Suzanne sat down on a bench outside the courtroom while Jeff got them sodas from the vending machine downstairs in the lobby.

"I can't believe it was that fast," said Suzanne, fanning herself with her purse.

"I know," Casey replied, her throat dry. "I wonder how long it will take them to decide."

"Soon. I think it will be soon," Suzanne said. "Your father didn't have much to say in his defense. Neither did his lawyer. I don't think it will take them long."

Just then, the side doors to the wide hallway burst open and a crowd of people rushed in loudly. There were men and women in dark suits carrying cell phones, tablets, and TV cameras. Lights flashed as they scurried after the two uniformed policemen who were escorting someone into the next courtroom.

Casey gasped. "It's Eric." She clutched Suzanne's hand. He was only several feet away, handcuffed, and heavily guarded. The reporters continued to call out their questions, but neither Eric nor the policemen made any effort to respond.

Eric met Casey's eyes briefly as they hurried him down the corridor. He stared blankly, refusing to recognize her.

Waves of relief broke over Casey as the guards disappeared with him into the adjacent courtroom, slamming the doors behind them. The reporters remained behind, frustration and disappointment showing on their faces. Casey sank back down onto the bench and rubbed her neck with both hands.

Jeff practically ran over to them with the soda. "What was all that commotion?" he asked, handing them each a drink.

"It was Eric," Casey said. "The reporters wanted him to make a statement, but he wouldn't. He's in there." She pointed toward the courtroom. "They just shut the doors behind him."

Jeff raised his soda can to Casey's in a celebratory toast. "Well then, here's to closed doors!"

CHAPTER 16

It is opening night of Godspell *and Casey peeks out from behind the dark red stage curtain. People are starting to fill the rows of metal folding chairs, fanning themselves with the beautiful programs that Jeff designed. She sees her mother and Grandma Rachel walk in and sit in the second row on the left. Chris's family is sitting in a cluster in the middle, and Suzanne's parents are also there, along with many others from the church and community.*

Someone tugs at her bright green scarf and she turns, facing Peter. "Hey you, get away from the curtain!" he says with a smile. "Come meet my daughter, the newest member of the Wright family!"

She quickly joins the others who are gathered around Marianne and the small bundle in her arms. "Angelica," they all croon to the little baby from Brazil. She is so tiny, so perfect.

Neil hands Peter a flat box, gift-wrapped and embellished with a soft pink bow which practically covers the box. "We got this for you. A baby welcoming gift," he says, winking at the others. He straightens the checkered golf cap which sits on his head, tucks in his bright red shirt and adjusts the lapels of his plaid jacket.

Peter tears off the paper, places the bow on Marianne's head, and opens the box. He pulls out a small white T-shirt, on which the words "Just Wright" have been carefully embroidered. He and Marianne burst into laughter. "This is perfect, guys, just perfect!" he exclaims. "Thank you!"

"We figured a daughter of yours is never too young to start wearing T-shirts!" says Neil, and they all laugh.

"I don't know if I can put her down long enough to play the piano for you guys," says Marianne, looking tenderly at Angelica.

"Well, you'd better, or we're all going to be in a lot of trouble," says Abby with a grin, smoothing her bright red overalls and rainbow suspenders.

Casey studies herself in one of the full-length mirrors in the Sunday School classroom which has been converted into the girls' dressing room. Her guitar is gripped tightly in her hands, and Friend the leopard peers out of the front pocket of her soft green pantaloons which billow out around her hips and then taper down to the elastic at her bare ankles. Her coppery red hair is loose around her shoulders and contrasts brightly with the green scarf flung carelessly around her shoulders. The blouse of dancing animals feels soft against her skin.

She smiles through the make-up which covers her freckles and grins at Kate, dressed in baggy paint-spattered overalls and a red checked blouse, who passes behind her and says knowingly, "Nice flowers, Casey!"

She touches the bright yellow buttercups and soft purple violets that her mother has twisted into a circlet on her head. It is held down with bobby pins, and Casey hopes it will last for the whole performance.

"Places, everyone," *calls Peter, clapping his hands for their attention. They hurry toward the back of the now-darkened hall. Casey bumps into Jeff as she takes her place beside him, waiting for the opening music. He wears baggy shorts cinched at the waist with frayed rope, and a white, poet's shirt, handpainted with violets and buttercups. It looks beautiful against his dark hair and gray eyes.*

Jeff gently touches the flowers in her hair and points to the flowers on his shirt. They smile at one another, enjoying the secret. She can see the smile, even though the hall is still dark. "Break a leg," *he whispers, his lips close to her ear.*

"Break a leg yourself," *she whispers back as the stage lights come on, and the music begins to play.*

Journaling & Discussion Questions

Read through the questions below and choose a few to write about in your journal or discuss with your friends or Youth Group.

1. Which character in *Come As You Are* can you relate to most? Why?

2. Imagine a picture similar to the one that Peter Wright gave the youth group: all those children on the playground. Which one is most like you?

3. What were the strengths and weaknesses of each of the main characters? Be sure to include Peter and Marianne in your comments. Is it okay for adults to have weaknesses as well as strengths? Why or why not?

4. Have you ever seen the musical *Godspell*? If so, what is your favorite scene or song? Why is it your favorite?

5. Why do you think the author named this book *Come As You Are*? What did this idea mean to Casey? To Jeff? To Peter and Marianne? To Chris? To Chris's grandfather?

6. What does the phrase "come as you are" mean to you? Do you have a place or places where you can show up exactly as you are and find acceptance? If so, describe that place/those places and what it is

about them that invites acceptance. If not, what action steps can you take to find a place that welcomes you as you are?

7. Marianne shares about a time in her life when she experienced fear. She says that she prays, and then she takes some kind of action. Think of a fear you currently have or have had recently. What would happen if you allowed yourself to feel the fear as you prayed about it and then chose to do something to move you forward and away from the fear?

8. Why did Casey change her mind about testifying at the court hearing against her father? Do you think she should have done something different?

9. *Come As You Are* is about welcoming and accepting others as much as we would like to be welcomed and accepted. Think about the people in your own life. Is there someone you could reach out to in order to make them feel more welcome?

10. If you could create a *Come As You Are* costume, what would it look like? What special pieces of clothing or accessories hold meaning for you that you would include?

Acknowledgements

The Community Center in Salem

It's hard for me to believe, but *Come As You Are* began in 1989 (way before you were born!). I was living alone in Salem, Massachusetts, and went to see a teen community center's production of *Godspell*. I have always loved musical theatre, but I'd never seen a show done entirely by teenagers. My imagination began stirring immediately as soon as the first act began. Who were those young men playing John the Baptist and Jesus? I wondered what had drawn them, and the other cast members, to *Godspell*. Did they believe the stories of Jesus that they were acting out? How did they create their unique costumes? Who was the leader that had put all of this together? What were their families like?

At one point, I remember taking out a small spiral notebook and taking notes (because, as you may know, a good writer always carries around a notebook and pen). I noticed a tall girl with long reddish-gold hair who seemed to have the light of Jesus around her, and I began to wonder if she was born with that light or if she had come to it through a difficult time in her life.

I can't remember the name of the community center, but I send gratitude out in waves to those young people (who are now middle-aged, yikes!) and their leaders who created such a spectacular version of a beloved musical.

Jeffrey

I worked on this book off and on over the years. At one point, my nine-year-old stepson Jeffrey walked into the room where I was writing and asked me what I was doing. I told him I was writing a book for teenagers.

"That's cool," he replied. "What's the title?"

When I told him it was *Come As You Are*, he immediately replied "Is it about God?"

I happily told him yes and that was the end of the conversation. I remember being really impressed that he understood enough about God to know that we are always welcomed exactly as we are. But now, so many years later, as I think back on this interaction, I am startled to realize that maybe Jeffrey did know God pretty well, but he also knew *me* pretty well.

So, thank you, Jeffrey, for being an important part of this book's creation.

Christian Youth Groups I Have Known and Loved

Throughout high school I was part of the CYO (Catholic Youth Organization) in my home parish of St. Bernard's Church in Rockville, Connecticut. When I was teaching second grade in Virginia, I was co-leader of the Christ Episcopal Church Youth Group in Amelia, Virginia, and I have the Reverend Donald Dunn to thank for roping me into that adventure! At a statewide youth retreat one year, we were given the black and white illustration of the children on the playground which plays such an important part of *Come As You Are*.

Blessings to you, Donald, for seeing something in me back then that I couldn't quite see.

And blessings also to whoever created that picture of the kids because it really made a difference in the teens I was working with (and yes, okay, me too).

St. Peter's Episcopal Church, Salem, Massachusetts

In 1991 I was Assistant Director in my home church's production of *Godspell*. This was one of the highlights of my life! Thank you to my friend and fellow theater geek, Lori Georgy, who trusted me with so many responsibilities. Thank you to every performer who depended on me for lines and notes. Thank you to the Reverend Randy Wilkinson, our rector at the time, for giving us permission to do the show and then cheering us on from beginning to end. This whole experience deepened my understanding of the meaning and importance of the *Godspell* message.

And mostly, thank you to the congregation of St. Peter's at that time (you know who you are!), for welcoming me with open arms several years prior to *Godspell*. You instilled in me the "come as you are" philosophy of accepting people exactly where they are on their journeys, and I will always be grateful.

Bookish Things

Thank you to the creative genius of Carol Coogan (www.carolcoogandesign.com) for the beautiful layout and cover design of this book. You have brought Casey and her story out of my dreams and into reality in such a thoughtful, relevant way.

Thank you to Lis Gordon who was my very first reader of the very first draft of *Come As You Are,* way back in 1993. I remember sitting with you over frozen yogurt one spring afternoon, eagerly receiving your comments and suggestions, all given to me with kindness and a deep shared love of reading and writing. Casey and Sunny's characters are much more evolved because of you. Even though you took your last breath in 2011, I hope that somewhere, somehow, you are able to celebrate the birth of this book (finally!) with me.

Thank you also to my early readers - Beverly Flanagan, Susan Nutting, and my nephew Mike Pacheco. It was great to bounce ideas off of all of you and to feel the encouragement of having this story received with such generous, loving hands.

Appreciation to the extremely competent OddballEditing over at Fiverr.com. Sorry, I don't know your real name, but you went through this manuscript with a fine-toothed and loving comb and it is a much better book because of you.

Last But Not Least

Dearest Jeff, I know that being married to a writer is not always the easiest thing because my mind is often somewhere else. You have encouraged me and supported me above and beyond the usual role of a husband, and I love you for that and for so much more.

About the Author

Anne Marie Bennett was born and raised in Connecticut. By the age of six, she could often be found in her room writing poems, journals, and stories (lots and lots of stories!). This passion for writing has been a bright thread tying together all the stages of her life, although now she more frequently uses a laptop and printer paper instead of all those multi-colored pens!

She graduated from Southern Connecticut State University in 1978 with a degree in Early Childhood Education, and from there moved to Amelia County, Virginia, where she taught second grade. In Amelia, she co-led the Christ Episcopal Church Youth Group for several years.

Anne Marie's career continued as an Educational Consultant and District Trainer for Jostens Learning Corporation. In 1991 she met her husband Jeff and took time off to help him raise the three children from his first marriage. Next, she worked part time as a substitute teacher, bookseller, computer teacher, and Assistant Box Office Manager at the North Shore Music Theatre. It is during this time period that *Come As You Are* was born.

Her life's path has also taken her through two journeys with cancer, once in 2002 and once in 2011. She is now cancer-free and happily back in her room writing stories, stories, and more stories!

Anne Marie is currently a SoulCollage® Facilitator and Trainer; she teaches this intuitive process of self-discovery (for teens and adults) online as well as in person at various workshop and retreat centers in the northeast. Her website is www.KaleidoSoul.com.

In the 90's, her essays were published by: *Living Streams, The Living Church, Today's Christian Woman, Instructor, Teaching and Computers, Christian Single,* and *Momentum.* Her novel for children, *My Other Dad,* was released in the spring of 1993 from Winston Derek Publishers (under her maiden name Anne M. Pacheco).

She has also published two books about her cancer journeys (*Bright Side of the Road,* and *Sunflower Spirit Workbook*) and three books about the SoulCollage® process (*Through the Eyes of SoulCollage®, Into the Heart of SoulCollage®,* and *Magical Inner Journeys*). These are all are available at Amazon.com.

Other interests include: reading, theatre, watercolor, mixed media art, making prayer beads, dancing, EFT Tapping, journaling, stitching, being loved up by her cats, hanging out with her grandchildren, and walking by the ocean to feel closer to God. She was raised in the Catholic faith, and is now a member of the Episcopal Church.

Anne Marie lives in eastern Massachusetts with her accountant husband Jeff and two adolescent cats, Louis and Seymour, who keep them all young at heart.

59455437R00093

Made in the USA
Middletown, DE
11 August 2019